DARK
WATERS

Jack Ross is a former journalist. His articles have appeared in newspapers including the *Daily Mail*, *Daily Telegraph*, *Scotsman*, *Daily Express* and *Herald*. He lives with his wife and two young children in Scotland.

Also by Jack Ross

Requiem

DARK WATERS

JACK ROSS

arrow books

Published by Arrow 2010

2 4 6 8 10 9 7 5 3 1

First published in Great Britain in 2010 by
Arrow Books
Random House, 20 Vauxhall Bridge Road,
London SW1V 2SA

www.rbooks.co.uk

Addresses for companies within The Random House Group Limited can be found at:
www.randomhouse.co.uk/offices.htm

The Random House Group Limited Reg. No. 954009

A CIP catalogue record for this book
is available from the British Library

ISBN 9780099520122

The Random House Group Limited supports The Forest Stewardship
Council (FSC), the leading international forest certification organisation. All our
titles that are printed on Greenpeace approved FSC certified paper carry the FSC logo.
Our paper procurement policy can be found at
www.rbooks.co.uk/environment

Typeset in Dante MT by Palimpsest Book Production Limited,
Grangemouth, Stirlingshire
Printed and bound in Great Britain by
CPI Cox & Wyman, Reading, RG1 8EX

For my Mother and Father

It started just before dawn.

The man stepped out of his home, unaware he was being watched. He stood on the dimly lit porch and stamped his feet against the November cold. He wore a cashmere coat over his suit and pulled on his leather gloves as he waited for his chauffeur. He looked just like any of the other prosperous Washington DC professionals in the neighborhood. But the observer peering through binoculars from a darkened attic room across the oak-tree-lined street – who'd tracked his movements for three months – knew different.

The observer knew that the man had one daughter, Elisabeth, who had been educated at the prestigious Holton-Arms girls' college prep school, along with the daughters of CEOs, diplomats, congressmen, and even presidents. Elisabeth was now nineteen and a law student at Georgetown University. The man visited her once a week. Afterwards, always drinking alone, he spent a couple of hours in Martin's Tavern sipping a few single malts, invariably Laphroaig, before his chauffeur drove him home.

That was his weak spot.

And tonight the observer would be waiting . . .

The smell of crab cakes and Angus steaks lingered in the air as the minutes ticked by while the observer waited for the man. Martin's Tavern was a Washington institution. It was situated in the heart of old Georgetown, a classic watering hole favored by the movers and shakers in the city. It exuded a timeless charm, its dark stained-wood paneling from a bygone age. That night it was packed, as usual, with journalists, politicians, and assorted hangers-on, drinking freely and talking loudly at their tables and booths.

The observer sat in a discreet hard-backed wooden booth. On the table in front of him lay his laptop and a Nokia Smartphone that he'd stolen from the handbag of the man's daughter less than three hours earlier at Mazza Gallerie, an upscale shopping mall in the suburb of Chevy Chase.

Suddenly, out of the corner of his eye, the observer saw the man walk in, shortly after seven p.m., as usual. No one seemed to notice. The man walked past tables of senators, their interns and Capitol Hill correspondents, hands thrust deep into the pockets of his expensive coat.

The observer stole a glance. He noticed the hand-stitching on the man's shiny black leather Italian shoes, his expensive suit underneath the coat, the clean shave, his thick neck and the bushy moustache. The man shook hands with Billy, the owner, before he was escorted, as he always was, to the Dugout room, a semi-private recess at the rear of the bar.

The observer was nursing a bottle of Schlitz, surreptitiously watching everything, just as he had for the last three months.

Thirty minutes later the man emerged from the Dugout and sat down on a stool at the mahogany bar where Billy poured him a malt whisky and water. The observer tried to listen in but the noise of the buzz, chatter and a Tony Bennett song playing in the background, was overpowering.

It was time.

The observer leaned forward and his eyes scanned the myriad wireless networks that his laptop had detected. There were sixty-two in the vicinity – not surprising – but the man's unusual surname jumped out at him.

Since he was within ten meters of his target, the observer wanted to see if he could, through a glitch in the Bluetooth wireless technology, access the data on the man's cellphone. It was an illegal hacking technique known as bluesnarfing which would enable him to make a wireless connection to the man's phone and transfer any data to his. But almost immediately his heart sank. The man's phone was switched to 'undiscoverable' mode, which meant that it would be nearly impossible in such a short time to hack in.

The observer didn't panic.

He took another sip of beer and picked up the stolen phone. This was his back-up plan. Then he sent a text message to the man's BlackBerry. It read, 'Hi dad, don't work too late.'

Immediately, the man nursing the malt at the end of the

bar lifted up his BlackBerry and looked at the message. Then a rueful smile crossed his face and he winked at Billy. He put his phone away, unaware of the deception.

Unbeknown to the man at the bar, a Trojan virus, Wipeout, which the observer had developed with a Finnish hacker, had been downloaded and would send the password on the man's phone back to his daughter's Nokia.

The password quickly appeared on the screen in front of him. CLANDESTINE.

The observer's heart was pounding hard as he keyed in the password and gained immediate access to hundreds of the man's confidential e-mails. He sent these to his laptop.

Satisfied that he had what he wanted, he shut the laptop, picked up the smartphone and walked out of the bar.

Once out of the door, the observer strode down Wisconsin and into the freezing night. He afforded himself a smile. After three months' close surveillance, one of the United States's most senior CIA agents had just been hacked by a twenty-year-old college student.

1

A molten sun burned above the horizon, its tangerine rays flooding across Biscayne Bay, igniting a new dawn in Miami. The light sparkled on the waters below like millions of mirrors, glass towers in the distance gleaming all around. It was mid-November, and the beaches would be filling up as they always did, the blazing heat forcing the sun worshippers to cool off among the Atlantic breakers by afternoon.

Traffic on the MacArthur Causeway heading downtown was moving well, the traffic to the beach virtually non-existent. That would change as tourists, day trippers and locals invaded South Beach across the water as temperatures soared into the nineties.

Deborah Jones sighed as she glanced east out of the *Miami Herald*'s fifth-floor newsroom. It was the start of another week. And it wasn't even seven o'clock. Her schedule was punishing and seemed to stretch ahead forever; assignments, investigations and articles blurred from one month to the next.

She picked up that morning's *Herald*, which was sitting on top of her in-tray, and began reading her team's latest hard-hitting exposé. It was an undercover investigation of cops taking kickbacks from pimps and drug dealers who worked the fenced-off area around the demolished and once-notorious Scott Carver housing project in Liberty City. It was a typical article for her team. Corruption seemed to be endemic – from poorly paid police officers taking bribes to turn a blind eye, to high-ranking politicians with handsome holiday homes on the Gulf Coast being rewarded for backing controversial new developments encroaching on the Everglades. And to cap it all there was the dirty money, especially from Latin America, which flowed through financial networks in and around Miami. Money laundering was an increasing problem because of the glut of huge banks in the city. Significant amounts of money, including Colombian, were held in deposits for international customers who nobody knew and who had private bank accounts. Since 2004 this had resulted in nineteen banks facing sanctions from federal regulators who found dirty dollars in the bank vaults of South Florida.

It sometimes seemed as if everyone was on the take. Perhaps her work had made Deborah more cynical over the years.

She heard Frank Callaghan shout from across the newsroom and she snapped out of her reverie. 'Got a wife of one of the corrupt cops on the line for you, Deborah. She's real pissed at today's story.'

'Thanks, Frank. Just what I need first thing on a Monday morning.'

He transferred the call and she picked up the phone. 'Is this the investigations editor I'm speaking to?' The caller was a Hispanic-sounding woman.

'Yes, how can I help?'

'Do you know what you've done to my family? Do you?'

'Who am I speaking to?'

'Caprice Gomez, wife of Sergeant Jesus Gomez of Miami-Dade Police Department.'

Deborah closed her eyes for a moment.

'Who do you think you are, huh? My husband barely earns enough to keep us. But you, sitting up there in your fancy office building, think you can libel anyone you want to. My husband is innocent.'

'Ma'am, I'm sorry.'

'Are you? Are you really sorry? Do you know my kids are crying this morning, not wanting to go to school, because of this story? You've wrecked our lives.'

'I'm truly sorry. But it's your husband who's been taking kickbacks.'

'You have no idea what he's like. He's a good man. He's worked hard all his life.'

'That's as maybe. But the last thing Liberty City needs, or Miami for that matter, is another corrupt police officer.'

'You know nothing. I hope you rot in hell, you bitch.' The woman hung up.

Deborah leaned back in her seat and watched the sun edge higher in the flawless early-morning sky. Then she closed her eyes.

'Hey, Deborah, another happy customer?'

Deborah saw Frank sitting on the corner of the desk opposite, a desk usually occupied by Rico Miralles, a talented new member of the investigations team. She raised her gaze to the ceiling.

Frank smiled. 'Bending your ear?'

'Chewing it off, more like.'

'Can't blame her.' He sat down in the seat opposite. 'I used to get that kind of abuse all the time when I covered the courts. The wives were always the worst because they didn't accept what had happened and why their husband's picture had to appear in the paper.'

'I feel sorry for her.'

Frank smiled and paused for a few moments. 'You're looking tired, Deborah. Take my advice: disappear for a couple of weeks. Recharge the batteries. And try and persuade Sam to go with you. For both your sakes.'

'We were supposed to be going away to Bermuda in July, but his sister's still recovering from a nasty stomach bug. It's like a post-viral thing now. She's exhausted all the time. Won't be dashing back to Egypt in a hurry, that's for sure. And Sam's a worrier anyway – you know how he is. But I guess that comes with the territory.'

Frank got to his feet. 'A word to the wise, Deborah. Take a break soon. It'll do you the world of good.'

Late that afternoon, Deborah drove back across MacArthur Causeway to her condo overlooking the beach, her thoughts turning again to the vast workload she faced. She wondered if Frank wasn't right.

It would do both her and Sam a power of good. Perhaps they should head up to Wyoming where Lauren lived, and enjoy the snow and the fresh cold air. Perhaps seeing Sam again would boost his sister's spirits.

Fifteen minutes later, Deborah was safely ensconced at home where the smell of fresh orange and beeswax furniture polish still lingered in the air. The new housekeeper was a godsend, allowing Deborah the rest of the evening to herself, the cleaning, dishes, washing and ironing all done. It might feel decadent, but she worked for it.

After soaking in a bath she lay back on the sofa, gazing at a picture on her mantelpiece. It showed her, Sam and his sisters together with their husbands at a Mexican restaurant in South Beach. It had been taken shortly after she'd unearthed the remarkable story of William Craig, the Death Row Scot, who was a war hero and had been freed in an eleventh-hour reprieve by the governor. That was her proudest moment in journalism. A photograph of Craig, taken outside his home in Scotland by his granddaughter, was in a gold frame on top of Deborah's TV. Craig wore a pure white shirt, a tightly knotted dark blue tie and a dark suit. His face was pale and kind and he was smiling broadly at the camera. In the background was a beautiful beach which seemed to go on for miles – Belhaven. Craig was eighty-seven, but he looked like a man fifteen years younger. It was as if his strength and spirit had been restored now that he was back in his home town, Dunbar, a free man, enjoying the winter years of his life in peace.

Deborah's phone rang and she looked at the clock on the wall. It was six o'clock precisely. She knew who it was.

'Hi, Momma.'

'You sound tired, honey. Are you sleeping okay?'

'I'm sleeping fine. Just work, you know.'

'Was telling your father that you work too hard. You need to take time out.'

'You sound just like one of the guys at the paper.'

Deborah felt she needed to prove herself over and over again. She still felt insecure. And, perhaps most of all, she still felt she had to prove herself to Sam, who was not only her boyfriend but also – as the *Herald*'s managing editor – her boss. Her team garnered awards and plaudits by the month, but the constant stress was taking its toll.

'You and Sam planning a visit at Thanksgiving?'

'I'm not too sure, although I'm sure Sam would love that.'

'Your father likes him a lot, you know.'

'What about you?'

'He's a smart, good-looking man, I'll give you that. But . . .'

Deborah said nothing, waiting for the punchline.

'But he's a good deal older than you, honey.'

'What's that supposed to mean?'

'And he was married before.'

'So?'

'So, you weren't his first love. I was your daddy's first love. And he was mine.'

'Sam and I are very happy.'

'So why don't you settle down?'

Deborah took a few moments to compose herself, fearing that she would say something she'd regret. 'Listen, we'll do things in our own good time. As it happens, we've talked about it, but . . .'

'But what?'

'Look, I don't think I need to explain myself. We've just not got round to it.'

'Please come for Thanksgiving. That's all I ask. It would make your father very happy.'

'How is he?'

'The same. Cantankerous to a fault.'

'Be patient with him.'

'Patient? I've been nothing but patient with that man for nearly fifty years.'

Deborah laughed. Her mother had tended to her father, a retired Baptist minister, since they'd first met on a Civil Rights march in the 1960s. They'd been inseparable ever since, even after his stroke had affected his speech. It frustrated him terribly, and occasionally he took his anger out on her mother. 'I gotta go. Can I let you know nearer the time?'

'Sure thing, honey. But please try. Love you.'

Deborah got up from the sofa and walked out onto the balcony overlooking the hustle and bustle of Collins below and onward to the Atlantic. The sun was low in the darkening sky. And the air was warm and sticky, the humidity suffocating despite it being November.

This was her home. Miami. High up in the sky, living alone, seeing Sam for lunch and weekends at his home, soccer with the girls on Tuesday evenings for practice and Saturdays for games.

She loved her work. But she wanted more out of life. She wanted to live with Sam, despite her mother's disapproval. More than anything she wanted to commit to Sam. But the truth was that physical intimacy still scared her. Sam seemed to understand and was content to let things take their course. Usually they lay down together, holding each other tight, but both of them afraid to make a move.

Deborah knew their set-up sounded strange, and some of her girlfriends on the soccer team laughed about it.

Occasionally she felt as though she was ready to take the plunge and seal their relationship by making love. But then the dark memories would resurface: the leering faces of the boys from Berkeley who'd raped her were still imprinted on her mind, and the deep longing to consummate their relationship would pass.

But she knew it couldn't go on.

Deborah imagined holding a baby – their baby. Sam had no children, and she knew he really wanted to be a dad.

Her home phone rang. She picked it up, wondering if it was Sam, if he was finishing early at the newsroom.

'Hello?'

There was no reply but she could sense someone at the other end.

'Who's this?'

A long pause before a young man's hesitant answer. 'Is that Deborah Jones of the *Miami Herald*?'

'I'm sorry, who is this?'

'I'd rather not give my name, if it's all right with you.'

'Do I know you?'

'Not personally, although I think we've met.'

Deborah felt ill at ease. She'd been receiving threatening calls lately from a man who usually called her office when he was drunk. What worried her was that only a handful of people, close friends, knew her home phone number.

'You come highly recommended by Sam.'

'You know Sam?'

'He knows me. Has done for years.'

'Did Sam give you this number?'

'No.'

'So how did you get it?'

'I hacked into your phone company's computer network.'

'Okay, that's it. I'm going to hang up—'

'No – listen, don't do that. As I said, Sam knows me, but I can't talk to him about what I know because he will tell my parents.'

'Is this some sort of joke?'

'This is no joke, believe me. Miss Jones, I haven't got too much time . . . Look, I've gotten hold of something.'

'So why are you coming to me?'

'You have a first-rate reputation.'

'What exactly are you talking about?'

'Encrypted government secrets. Files so secret you won't believe. E-mails. Protocols. I have it all.'

Deborah didn't respond.

'Look, all I want to do is show you these files.'

'Why don't you send them to the paper, marked for my attention? Or send them to Sam.'

'I don't believe they will reach either of you if I send them by mail.'

Deborah thought he sounded totally paranoid. 'Well, e-mail them, then.'

'Miss Jones, I need to know that you have the documents in person.'

'Look, I'm kinda busy, why don't we—'

'Do you know Dadeland Mall?'

'I don't even know who you are. Why would I—'

'Please listen to me. And trust me. Sam really does know me.'

'I only have your word for it.'

'Meet me at Dadeland Starbucks tomorrow lunchtime,

at midday, when it's nice and busy. Everything will become clear. But come alone. And don't tell a soul. Not even Sam. That's important.'

'I think I'm going to hang up.'

'All I ask is to see you, to hand over these documents. You won't be sorry.'

'What if I don't turn up?'

A long silence ensued before the young man spoke again. 'I think you will.'

2

When she awoke the next morning Deborah still hadn't got the young man's voice out of her head. He sounded educated, with a hint of Florida twang, but most of all he sounded genuine.

In many ways it should have been an easy decision to make. She should just have forgotten the call. Besides, if she was to head out to the mall, she was supposed to heed the paper's safety guidelines for journalists and tell a colleague where she was going, and why.

Just after eight a.m. Deborah called Rico, one of her investigations team, to tell him that she wouldn't be in until that afternoon because she was working from home. If anyone needed to contact her they should try her cellphone. Like most inquisitive journalists Rico asked what she was working on, but she just said that she needed to tie up some loose ends concerning the police-corruption investigation that had dominated the previous day's *Herald*.

By 10.30 a.m. she was alone in her Mercedes convertible, driving back across the causeway, shades on, the radio playing a manic Latino song, as the wind whipped up the dark blue waters of Biscayne below.

Deborah loved Miami, especially South Beach. It was now her home, a tropical, concrete, man-made paradise of high-rise condos and Art Deco hotels, built right in the middle of what had once been a wilderness – a sandbar infested with rat snakes, poisonous cottonmouths and mosquitoes.

She turned away from the *Herald*'s building overlooking Biscayne and onto I-95 S and then to the South Dixie Highway, past Coral Gables, heading in the direction of Dadeland Mall in the suburb of Kendall.

Her cellphone rang. It was Leroy Johnston, her deputy on the investigations team. 'Hey, Deborah, Rico was telling me you won't be attending the morning news meeting. Is that right?'

'I'm afraid so. Can you sit in for me?'

'Not a problem.'

'Thanks, Leroy. There's a red file on my desk which should have everything you need.'

'But anything I ought to be aware of before Sam starts firing questions at me?'

Deborah laughed. 'The housing-agency scandal is ongoing. Rico's on top of that, and you're doing sex offenders working in Miami-Dade schools. How's that shaping up?'

'Talk about depressing. I've uncovered at least two teachers, both of whom underwent Board of Ed background checks. You believe that?'

'Nothing surprises me anymore.'

Deborah spotted the modernist main entrance of the Dadeland Mall, fringed by palms, and turned off the expressway. 'Is there anything else?'

'That's it, Deborah. I'll catch up with you later.'

She ended the call and pulled up at the parking lot by Firestone Tires. She got out of her car, briefcase in hand, and did what she usually did. She checked her reflection in a side window; she was looking smart in the new black Prada suit she'd bought on Washington Avenue the previous week. Her obsession with always dressing the part came from her father, who wouldn't leave their house in Jackson without a starched white shirt, immaculate suit and clerical collar, and black shoes polished to a deep shine. He thought it was about pride. Pride in one's appearance gave one pride in oneself, and it fostered respect.

Deborah was early, so she took her time and did some desultory window shopping. She had at least an hour to kill before midday.

She wondered if the mystery caller wasn't already in the mall, watching her movements from afar.

The smell of scented candles wafted out of a shop, then the aromas of warm chocolate and, finally, coffee.

Deborah saw the Starbucks sign and the kiosk, a handful of tables and the distinctive dark green umbrellas. No one else was there.

She ordered a cappuccino and a blueberry muffin and sat down to read that day's *Herald*, wondering if and when her mysterious caller would make an appearance.

3

Sam Goldberg leaned back in his leather chair in his office in the *Herald* building, his right shirtsleeve rolled up, a blood-pressure cuff wrapped round his upper arm. It was his annual check-up.

'No difference from the last time,' Dr Manny Epstein said, loosening the cuff.

Sam winced.

'Borderline dangerous.'

'But I don't drink any more.'

'That's good. But what about exercise? What about your workload?'

'My work is my exercise.' Sam stood up. 'You know how it is.'

Dr Epstein carefully stored the blood-pressure kit in his black bag. 'Listen to me, Sam. We've known each other for a long time. But no one's immortal. Now, I really am delighted you quit drinking, but you need proper exercise. Walk on the beach, have a swim, spend some time with your girlfriend. Don't get so fixated on your damned paper.'

Sam rolled down his shirtsleeve and did up the button.

'You don't win any prizes when you're six feet under.'

Sam gave a wry smile. 'I must remember to mention that to my executive editor when he's going over the circulation figures.'

After the doctor had gone, Sam reflected that it was all very well being blasé in your twenties. But once he'd hit forty, and certainly when he'd lost his wife, he'd felt increasingly conscious of his own mortality.

There was a knock at the door and Frank Callaghan walked in. 'Got a minute, Sam?'

'Sure.' Sam slumped back in his seat and Frank sat in a matching leather chair on the other side of the desk.

'You're not gonna like this. I've just heard from the new guy on Investigations . . .'

'Rico.'

'Yeah, that's right, Rico. Look, I don't want you to overreact but . . .'

'Spit it out, Frank.'

'Apparently Deborah has been receiving threatening phone calls.'

'Related to one of her investigations?'

'We don't know, but she's stepped on quite a few toes. Cops, pimps, politicians, you name it.'

'So why are you only telling me now?'

'I only just heard it myself. What worries me is that

this guy, according to Rico, has also threatened to have her killed.'

'Did he cite any articles?'

Frank shook his head.

'No wonder I've got fucking high blood pressure. I'm telling you, Frank, I'm going to have some words with her. I need to know these things, goddamit.'

Sam glanced up at the TV. CNN was showing the aftermath of a car bombing in Iraq. 'I know it's not your fault,' he said to Frank, 'but I don't want to hear about death threats second-hand.'

Sam's eyes flicked back to the TV. Burning cars, pools of blood, screaming people, smoke billowing into the Baghdad sky.

4

Harry Donovan, executive editor of the *Miami Herald*, donned his sunglasses as he stepped onto Crandon Beach's white sands, his son, Andrew – carrying a new Adidas soccer ball – by his side. Under his left arm Harry carried an icebox, a blanket under his right. In the icebox were dozens of ham sandwiches that he'd made up earlier, packed neatly in Tupperware boxes, along with five huge bottles of still water.

'Now remember, plenty of sunblock like Mom said, okay?'

Andrew rolled his eyes. 'Dad, gimme a break. You sound like my teacher.'

'Hey, I'm not joking. It's gonna be high eighties today.'

'Whatever.'

Harry picked a shaded spot under a clump of huge palms, partially shielded from the blistering sun. He put down the blanket. Then he smeared the sun cream over his son's face, torso and legs before he adjusted the junior Miami Dolphins baseball cap.

'Go play,' Harry said.

He experienced a surge of happiness as Andrew kicked the ball down the beach. He was lucky if he saw his son once a week. This was a rare day off for Andrew from his private school, Random Everglades School in Coconut Grove. The boy, his spitting image with wavy brown hair and dark brown eyes, occasionally turned round and grinned at his dad, showing off his newly acquired soccer skills. And all around, scores of families as far as the eye could see, some Latino, some as white as the sand they were playing on, chilled out, ate picnics, listened to some music, or stared out at the pale blue waters off Key Biscayne.

Sweat trickled down Harry's back, dampening his white linen shirt.

This beach was a favorite of his, the pace and ambience a far cry from the touristy haunts of South Beach. Crandon was regularly named among the top ten in the US, and it was safe, protected by an offshore sandbar. Nevertheless, lifeguards kept watch from thirteen elevated towers along the two-mile stretch.

Andrew dropped the ball at Harry's feet and wrapped his arm around him. 'Dad, can I tell you something?'

'Course you can.'

'I don't know if I should say . . .'

'Say what?'

'Well, Mom has met someone. She showed me a picture of him.'

Harry smiled and stroked his son's hair. 'I know, she told me. Look, Andrew, you've got a great mom and she's entitled to a life, just like I am.'

'Don't you love her?'

'Of course. But it's complicated.'

'Dad, I don't want to meet this new man. I just want to be with you.'

'Andrew, what have I always said?'

Andrew shrugged.

'Didn't I say that I'll always be your dad, no matter what?'

Andrew nodded, but there was confusion in his eyes. 'Come on,' Harry said. 'I'll be in goal. Penalty shoot-out.'

And then his cellphone rang.

Checking the caller display, his heart sank. It was Juan Garcia, the paper's publisher, making his daily call from somewhere in Peru where he was hiking along some ancient Inca trail.

'We need to talk, Harry.' The line was cutting up. 'I can't go on with Sam acting the way he is.'

'Juan, I'm not in the office today. Long weekend. Remember?'

Juan took no notice. 'I will not stand for Sam's insubordination much longer. Who the hell does he think he is? Five minutes ago I mentioned, really nicely, that he still hadn't come up with sufficient savings in the newsroom. Ten per cent is all. And you know what he said?'

'I've got a fair idea.'

'He told me that the newspaper was as lean as he

could make it without compromising quality. Harry, that's complete bullshit, and he knows it. The newspaper industry is facing tough times and we've gotta reduce the workforce. It's painful but essential. He knows as well as I do that it can be done by eliminating open positions and voluntary buyouts. Shit, we have a really generous severance package.'

'Let's go over the plans, line by line, next week.'

'But that's what we did last month. And the month before that. I'm banging my head against a brick wall here.'

'Look, cutbacks are a very sensitive area. But I agree with you, savings can be made. I'll have a word with him.'

'Set up a meeting for the day I get back. I want this resolved before the holidays.'

Juan hung up.

'Sorry, Andrew,' Harry said. 'I'll be with you in a moment.' He dialed another number while his son attempted to keep the ball in the air with his right foot. 'You okay to talk, Sam?'

'Thought you were putting your feet up on the beach.'

'I'm trying. Look, Juan's not happy. We need to resolve the rationalization issue once and for all.'

'He called you on your day off for that? Is he nuts?'

'I'm serious, Sam. We have to cut costs.'

'Not at the expense of the paper. Shit, they're even talking about outsourcing archiving and the production of the international edition to India. What the hell is that all about?'

'We both know that Juan has got this figure of ten per cent in his head, so we've just got to deal with that, okay? The figures I showed you the other week for advertising revenue are grim. It's time to get real. In the past we've avoided large-scale layoffs, I know, but things are different now.'

'He's an asshole, Harry. I've said it before and I'll say it until I'm blue in the face. He is not a proper newspaperman. He doesn't know what it's like.'

'He wants the paper to succeed.'

'We all want the paper to succeed. But I can't allow him to destroy everything we've built up just so he can satisfy the shareholders. I'm not accountable to them.'

'But you're accountable to me. Look, this problem is affecting everybody. The *New York Times* and *Washington Post* have been wielding the axe. We aren't entitled to any special dispensation.'

There was a long sigh at the other end of the phone.

'Look, we'll go over the figures tomorrow, first thing. Okay? Let's sort this out.'

'Enjoy the rest of your day, Harry.'

Down the beach, Andrew tried an ambitious overhead kick, missing the ball entirely. He fell flat on his back in the sand and burst out laughing.

Harry ran over to his son and pinned him on his back before tickling him on his stomach. Andrew convulsed with hysterical laughter as he always did. Then Harry hauled the boy to his feet and hugged him tight.

At that moment his gaze was drawn to a glint of light

further along Crandon's pristine beach. It took him a few seconds as he shielded his eyes from the sun to figure out what it was.

Partially concealed by an observation tower and some palm trees a man was crouched, pointing a huge tele-photo lens at them.

5

It was 12.01 p.m. and still no sign of the mystery caller. Deborah ordered another cappuccino and wondered if she hadn't been the victim of a practical joke.

Looking around, she saw families, office workers in suits having an early lunch, wealthy suburban women sporting deep tans, bedecked in gold and laden with shopping bags full of designer clothes, iPods and Belgian chocolates.

Her cellphone rang at 12.03 p.m. and she picked up immediately.

'We've got a problem.' It was him. Voice taut as a piano wire.

'Listen, if you're wasting my time—'

'Please don't hang up. I have reason to believe that there are police or Feds here. I'm scanning their frequencies as we speak. They're watching you. Right now.'

Deborah could not see anything or anyone untoward.

'Look, I'm sorry, but I can't take chances.'

'Where are you?'

'Nearby. I watched you arrive and do some window shopping before you sat down to read the paper. You bought a cappuccino and a muffin.'

'Now you're beginning to creep me out.'

'How difficult do you think it would be for me to hack into Dadeland's security systems and see what their cameras see?'

Deborah looked up and saw a camera pointing straight at her. 'You're watching me now?'

'You're wearing a nice watch, silver face. I didn't mean to scare you, but I can't take any chances. I've got the files and I wanted to hand them over in person, but as it stands that can't happen today.'

'Well, I guess there's not much point in me sitting around, then.'

'I tried calling you earlier to talk to you, but your cellphone was switched to voicemail.'

'I never switch my cellphone to voicemail unless I'm in an important meeting.'

'Then it looks like someone has managed to get into your cell system.'

'Now you sound real crazy.'

'Trust me, someone has accessed your cellphone company's computers and started tampering with your settings. I switched it back so I could make this call.'

'Why don't you just e-mail me?'

'Do you know how easy it would be for the NSA to block that and trace me?'

Deborah finished her cappuccino. 'Perhaps the NSA is listening in to this call. What do you think?'

The young man sighed. 'Look, I am not a conspiracy nut. I met you once at a party.'

'Well, I don't remember you. What do we do now? Until you give me something—'

'We're talking about national security. And the people who are supposed to be protecting us. I'm on the fucking run and my life is on the line. Do you understand that?'

'Why me? Why not someone at the *Washington Post* or the *New York Times* if it's such an important story? How did you get hold of these files?'

There was a long pause. 'It's called social engineering. If you were a hacker you'd know.'

'Okay, let's say you're telling me the truth. Just get the files to me. Can you do that?'

'I'm sorry. I have to go now. I'll be in touch.'

The line went dead.

6

An hour later, feeling tense and irritable after sitting in an endless traffic jam on the South Dixie Highway, Deborah finally got back to the newsroom.

Rico had managed to secure an exclusive interview with a former employee of the disgraced Miami-Dade Housing Agency. Her team had checked hundreds of project files, federal records, letters from construction firms, and the housing agency's financial accounts, and had uncovered a shocking scandal.

Multimillion-dollar contracts had been handed out to developers to demolish run-down old homes in exchange for building new ones. Years later, people had lost their poor-quality older accommodation and next to nothing had been built to rehouse them.

On Miami's northwest side the developers had planned to demolish the barracks-style homes of the Scott Carver housing project and construct more townhouses and single-family accommodation in the area. But all there was to show for it was a vacant wasteland, rubble and boarded-up buildings. While this was a classic case of investigative journalism, the poor in the city still ended up with a pile of dirt, broken dreams and shattered lives.

Just after five p.m., Deborah's cellphone rang.

It was Sam. 'Fancy a bite to eat?' He sounded weary.

'Hey, where are you?'

'The usual place.'

'I thought you were supposed to be heading up to Wyoming tonight?'

'I was, but you know how it is.'

'And you want me to drop what I'm doing, right now?'

'The fresh air'll do you good.'

Half an hour later Deborah was picking at her pasta in the late-afternoon sun outside the News Café on Ocean Drive. Sam had ordered a bottle of San Pellegrino but no wine. He smelled nice – he was wearing the Calvin Klein aftershave Escape – and was sporting an aqua Hugo Boss silk tie. She had bought both items for his birthday the previous Thursday. Deborah thought the tie matched the color of his eyes. She leaned over and kissed him on the lips.

Bass-heavy rap pumped out of a BMW cruising past. The driver, a black guy dripping with gold jewelry, stared belligerently back at them. On the sidewalk the usual assortment of beautiful people and weird South Beachers ambled past.

Stick-thin models with chiseled features and wearing skimpy hot pants chattered into their cellphones while they walked. Young Latin male models in low-slung jeans showed off their heavily tanned six-packs. Tourists soaked up the atmosphere, drank their beers and Pinot Grigio in the shade and watched the world go by.

'This is very unlike you,' Deborah said.

'Epstein told me to ease up a bit.'

'You don't normally take advice. I think we should do it more often.' She took a delicious mouthful of creamy mushroom pasta and sea bass. 'You're mad at me, aren't you? I can tell.'

Sam said nothing and gazed across Ocean Drive towards some kids playing volleyball in Lummus Park.

'What's wrong?'

'Why didn't you tell me about the telephone calls, Deborah?'

'He's just a screwball. Why should I worry you?'

'Who is he?'

'I don't know for sure. Maybe one of the guys from the housing agency.'

'Frank said you were working from home this morning.'

'That's not strictly correct.'

Sam shrugged.

'Look, I was supposed to meet up with some guy, some computer hacker, out at the Dadeland Mall. He said you knew him and that he'd met me before. But he didn't show. Think he got spooked.'

Sam touched the back of her hand as if to reassure her. It felt good. 'Did he give you a name?'

Deborah shook her head.

'Look at Sara Romeriz, a few years back,' Sam continued. 'She was like you. Good reporter. Ambitious. One night she decides to meet some guy who called the newsroom saying he had a story about the Miami chief of police and some prostitutes. She goes to a bar in Little Havana, and the guy tries to rape her in the parking lot. She was lucky. A couple of regulars knocked the shit out of him before the police arrived.'

Deborah fiddled with her pasta but didn't eat any more of it. 'So, if I had come to you this morning and told you that some guy who claimed to have hacked into my phone records had a hot story for me, what would you have got me to do differently?'

Sam puffed out his cheeks.

Deborah raised her glass of San Pellegrino. 'Cheers,' she said. On the horizon a huge cruise ship was leaving Miami, perhaps for the Caribbean. 'My mother wants us to come for Thanksgiving—'

'And that's supposed to help my blood pressure?'

Deborah laughed. 'How about we spend a couple of days there, then a couple of weeks in Barbados? The West Coast.'

'Book it and use my card.'

'I'll use my card, and we can split it. How does that sound?'

'I must be paying you too much.'

Sam's cellphone rang and he rummaged in his jacket, which was hanging over the back of his chair. 'Goldberg,' he said. He listened to the call for nearly a minute, before saying, 'I'll be right over.' He turned to Deborah 'Look, I'm sorry, that was an old friend of mine from college – Bill Hudson. Just got back from vacation to discover there's been a break-in at his home.'

'The lawyer, right?'

'Had us over just before Christmas. Remember?'

'Sure. Good party.'

Sam wiped his mouth with his napkin and stood up, putting on his sunglasses. 'I'm really sorry to cut this short. But please book the trip. Will you do that?' He bent down and kissed her on the cheek. 'I love you, you know.' He placed one hundred dollars under the ashtray. 'That should cover it.'

'Why don't you pop round for breakfast tomorrow?'

'Might just do that.'

Deborah smiled and watched him walk up Eighth Street where he usually parked his car. He turned and gave her a wave.

7

Nathan Stone pulled up at the neon-lit gas station and truck stop just off I-95 near Charlotte, North Carolina. Slowly he climbed out of his car and yawned. He hadn't slept for forty-eight hours.

Nathan Stone looked just like any of the other white guys milling around, stretching their legs after a long drive. He wore a baseball cap, black leather jacket over a white T-shirt, faded jeans and scuffed cowboy boots.

'Fill her up, son.' The attendant duly obliged, nervously wiping his oily hands on a rag. Nathan paid in cash, tipping the boy five dollars. Then he stepped into the restaurant where he took a window seat overlooking the parking lot. He flicked idly through the menu before ordering a coffee and pancakes.

After his meal he headed to the bathroom and splashed some cold water on his face. The smudged mirror reflected his chiseled, tanned features, thick neck and bulging veins. Nathan took half a dozen steroid pills from a little bag in his back pocket and washed them down with the lukewarm water from the tap. The steroids were a habit that had given him the edge since he was a teenager.

Five minutes later he was back in his car and back on the freeway, headed north, feeling the energy surge through his body. He was still five hundred miles from New York, a good nine-hour drive ahead. It was the city he'd grown up in – the Lower East Side, more than forty years ago. But this was no trip back home to see friends and family.

He sped on through the night, the headlights of cars and trucks flashing through his head. The road ahead was long. He'd traveled it a thousand times. He never took the plane. Too dangerous. Too many checks. Traveling on the freeways he was at liberty to move around uninterrupted, minding his own business.

He switched on his CD player, lit up a Winston and dragged the smoke deep into his lungs as the guitar riffs of the Georgia Satellites blared out of his speakers. He pressed his foot down on the accelerator and soon he was eating up the miles.

Nathan knew that when he arrived at his Times Square hotel he'd check in under a false name as he always did, not draw attention to himself, and retire to his room for the rest of the day.

When he woke it would be dark again. Then he'd wait some more. That was the way it was. That was the way it would always be. He didn't mind. He didn't have anywhere else to go.

Eventually his cellphone would ring. Nathan didn't know when that would be. That was their prerogative. That was the way they liked to work. But then a familiar low voice would give the name and address of a person he'd never met. He would scribble it down on a hotel pad, then hold his breath waiting for the four words:

Time to play, Nathan.

8

The sun was low in the sky when Deborah awoke. She heard whistling and soft music coming from the kitchen. She was pleasantly surprised to see Sam sitting on a stool at the counter skimming through that morning's *Herald*. Two fresh mugs of coffee, a pitcher of freshly squeezed orange juice and a plate of warm croissants were on the table. He had a key to her apartment and she had one to his house, so they could drop by each other's place whenever they felt like it.

Deborah kissed him on the cheek.

'Croissants are straight out of the oven from La Provence French Bakery fifteen minutes ago.'

Deborah took a bite. It was delicious. 'I'm impressed.' She took a gulp of hot coffee and felt the caffeine hit her system.

'So, how is your friend after the break-in?'

'Angry.'

'What did they take?'

'That's the funny thing. It's a four-million-dollar home, with jewelry and valuable paintings in it, and all they took were five hundred dollars from a bedside cabinet. And a laptop. Police were dusting for prints when I was there, but I don't think they found anything. And you know the other strange thing? No windows were broken or doors forced. And this place is in a gated community. So someone managed to evade their alarm system, security and cameras, and gain entry. Police are due to interview the housekeeper later this morning. She knew the house would be empty, and she's got a spare set of keys.'

'A big-shot city lawyer burgled by his housekeeper. Now that *is* a story. Didn't we do a profile of him last year?'

'That's right.'

'Maybe this is industrial espionage? Perhaps someone connected to a case he was working on?'

'I guess.'

Deborah wiped crumbs from her mouth and the grease from her hands with a paper napkin. Her phone rang and they groaned in unison. She let it ring for a few seconds, thinking it was probably one of her team, before picking it up.

'Deborah Jones.'

'Long time no hear, Miss Jones.' She recognized the voice immediately. It belonged to one of her most trusted sources, Emmett Ferrell.

Sam stood up, put on his jacket and waved to her. 'See you in the office,' he mouthed.

Deborah blew him a kiss as he walked out of the door. 'Hey, Emmett. What's going on?'

'I'm feeling neglected.'

'What do you want, exactly?'

'I want to talk.'

'You got a story?'

'Might have.'

'Look, Emmett, I don't have time to play games. You got something or not?'

'Sure. But not on the phone.'

'Where?'

'Usual place, half an hour.'

The diner on the corner of Washington and 11th Street was packed with bleary-eyed clubbers, tourists, and people like Emmett Ferrell who had just finished their shifts and had trouble sleeping.

Ferrell sat in a corner booth, sipping from a bottle of Red Stripe. He was heavily tanned, sported a short-sleeved white shirt and wore his usual dark mascara.

Emmett Ferrell worked at the city morgue and seemed to know everyone and everything. He lived in a tiny two-bedroom apartment on Drexel in South Beach which he'd inherited after his mother died. There was something creepy about him. His gaze lingered too long, the silences were too icy. When he wasn't working he hung out in gay bars, and he knew all there was to know about the darker side of the city. All he ever seemed to want from Deborah was a beer or two for his tips.

She'd used him for at least half a dozen stories concerning such matters as crooked cops earning kickbacks by turning a blind eye to drug dealing in clubs, and child sex slaves from Eastern Europe and the Middle East selling their bodies in brothels that were protected by Miami police.

She sat down in the booth opposite him. 'You're looking well.'

He rolled his bloodshot eyes. 'I've been up all night.'

Emmett was in his early forties. There was a sadness about him that was impossible to ignore. Deborah didn't know if it was because of the humiliation he had endured after being forced to resign from a previous job at the morgue in the Broward County Medical Examiner's Office in nearby Fort Lauderdale, hounded out by co-workers who were anti-gay. Or because he always seemed to be drinking, unable to look the real world in the eye. Or maybe it was just the nature of his job as a mortuary attendant, wheeling bodies to and from autopsies.

Deborah signaled to the waiter. She ordered a latte for herself and another beer, along with scrambled eggs and wheat toast, for Emmett.

'I'm not hungry,' he protested.

'It'll do you good.'

Emmett finished his beer.

'So, what's going on?' she asked. 'How's the love life?'

'Non-existent. But not for want of trying.'

'So, you got something for me?'

Emmett nodded. 'Yeah, believe I do.' He went quiet for a few moments, then said, 'I've been doing this job for many years, as you know, and I've seen a lot of bad things. Bodies torn to pieces, murder victims, suicides, young drive-by shooting casualties, overdoses, you name it.'

Deborah felt her foot begin to tap against the leg of the table.

'But you learn to deal with it,' Emmett said.

'You switch off, right?'

'I just do my job, take my paycheck, and get on with my life.'

Deborah waited patiently for him to get to the point.

'Just before I finished my shift we got a call to say that they were bringing in a body.'

The waiter returned with the food, beer and coffee. Emmett waited until the man was out of earshot before he spoke again. Deborah smelt his sour breath.

'A few hours ago, a partially dismembered body of a young white man was dragged out of the Everglades. Apparently some environmentalists were working nearby, studying the types of birds around at night or some shit like that. They came across the corpse, or most of it, floating in the water. But there was something very interesting, and I thought you should know about it. When I wheeled the body into the decomp room at the morgue I noticed some writing on the palm of his left hand.'

'What sort of writing?'

44

Emmett took a large swig of his Red Stripe.

'It was a telephone number.'

'That's not so peculiar.'

'The thing is, Deborah, I recognized it immediately. It was yours.'

9

Deborah rushed to the bathroom and only just made it into a stall before she was violently sick. For the next few minutes she crouched over the bowl, fearing that she would throw up again. But when she was satisfied the moment had passed she stood up gingerly and went over to the sink. After she had thrown some cold water over her face she felt a bit better.

Carefully, she reapplied her lipstick and fixed her smudged mascara. Then, taking a few deep breaths, she regained her composure and went back to join Emmett at his table. He'd ordered another beer for himself and a glass of water for her.

'You okay?' he asked.

Deborah drank some water. 'I've felt better.'

'Perhaps I shouldn't have told you.'

'Has the body been ID'd?'

Emmett nodded. 'Name John Hudson mean anything to you, Deborah? His father's a big-shot lawyer.'

Deborah felt her throat tighten.

The color drained from Sam's face when Deborah told him the news.

'Are you sure?' he asked.

'Called the cops on my way over here. They confirmed the name.'

'I see.' Tears filled his eyes.

'Sam, I'm sorry.'

'John Hudson was my godson.'

Deborah reached out and held his hand, squeezing it tight, but said nothing. 'I'm so sorry.'

He leaned back in his seat and closed his eyes. 'Bill's gonna be crushed by this news. John was the apple of his eye. MIT. Had the world at his feet. Computer whizz.'

'This hasn't been made official yet, Sam, but it's only a matter of time before this leaks out.'

'What else are the cops saying?'

'Off the record, they're talking about suicide, or maybe a drunken prank on an airboat that went wrong.'

'What do you think?'

Deborah shook her head. 'First a break-in at Bill's family home, then his son winds up dead. Sam, I think John was the hacker who was trying to contact me.'

10

The medical examiner's office in downtown Miami was all wood, fine carpets and brick. It looked more like a business headquarters than a facility that cut up dead bodies.

A female member of staff escorted Sam down to the morgue, which was located on the ground floor below the toxicology lab. It contained three suites. The first was the teaching room where students could watch an autopsy. The second was the main morgue with twelve autopsy stations. Sam was shown to the 'decomp' morgue that handled decomposed corpses or bodies with infectious diseases like TB and hepatitis.

Bill Hudson stood at the entrance with the Chief Medical Examiner. Bill's eyes were red. He stepped forward immediately and gave Sam a hug.

The Chief Medical Examiner introduced himself. 'Doctor Brent Simmons.'

'Sam Goldberg. I'm an old friend of Bill's.'

'Hard to believe it's my boy in there. The gators must've . . .' Bill's face crunched up. 'My beautiful boy.'

'Where's Kate?'

'Back at the house. I didn't want her to see this.'

'Do you mind if I . . . ?' Sam asked.

He was taken down a corridor into a small windowless room where he was given protective clothing, including a gown and mask, shoe covers and a clear plastic face shield.

'You sure about this?' Simmons asked.

Sam nodded. Heart pounding, he was escorted down yet another corridor, past the autopsy laboratory, then anthropology, before they arrived at the huge steel door of the walk-in cooler. He shivered at the sudden drop in temperature. The brown floor tiles were polished to a deep shine.

The metal storage racks were like huge filing cabinets.

'Holds seventy-five bodies.' Simmons pressed a button and an electronic forklift identified a rack, and a tray slowly emerged in front of them. Sam's nose wrinkled at the whiff of decay.

John's right leg had been severed just above the knee. His pale blue eyes were open, glassy and empty.

Had he tried to contact Deborah? Was he the one?

'The dark blood that has pooled on the deceased's face, chest and abdomen is because he was found face down in the water.'

Sam noticed the ingrained dirt around John's finger-nails. But there was no number written on either palm. *Had Deborah's source made it up? Then again, had someone scrubbed off the number? But who would do that?*

'Have you seen enough, Mr Goldberg?'

'Yes, thank you, doctor. Quite enough.'

Bill sat hunched in the passenger seat, head bowed, as Sam drove him back to his home in Coconut Grove.

'A couple of days ago Deborah was contacted by a young man who didn't identify himself but said he knew me.' Sam had decided to tell Bill everything. 'Apparently he had hacked into some sensitive government stuff. He wanted to meet up and talk. But he didn't make it. Called off at the last minute, saying his life was in danger. Do you think it could have been John?'

Bill said nothing, his eyes shut tight.

'We will have to run with this story. I'm sorry. At this stage we'll just say that a mystery surrounds the tragic death of a brilliant student. I'll make sure it's done properly.'

'I want you to do me a favor, though, Sam,' Bill muttered.

'Of course.'

'Find out what happened to my boy, do you hear me? What really happened? I need to know.'

11

The night air was like glue as Harry Donovan sat on an outside deck of the Miami Shores Country Club with his old newspaper buddy Ron Hirshman from the *Sentinel*. They were shooting the breeze after a formal charity fundraising dinner for a journalism scholarship, organized on behalf of the South Florida International Press Club.

'It ain't like it used to be,' Ron said, eyes twinkling, a large glass of red wine in his hand. 'Water from the cooler, that's all the kids in the newsroom drink now.'

Harry was nursing a near-empty glass of single malt. 'If they saw what we used to put away at lunch they'd run a mile.'

'In the old days I'd get back to the *Sentinel* after a three-bottler, file my story, then have a little stiffener before going home. What's happened to the world?'

'It got dull and boring and bureaucratic.'

'You remember that time I got my ass kicked when

Edna Buchanan beat me to that double suicide in Kendall, just three doors down from my home?'

'Man, she was good.'

'Good? The best. Edna was, without a shadow of doubt, a goddamn legend.'

'She still living in the city?'

'Where else? She'll never leave Miami. Bumped into her a few months back. Still as sharp as a knife.'

Harry nodded. 'Sam Goldberg reckons he learned more from Edna than he did from anyone at the paper.'

'How are things between you two?'

'Sam'll never change, you know what he's like. Law unto himself. But it's nothing I can't handle. The paper's better than it's ever been. But all the talk is about cutbacks and bottom line.'

Harry's cellphone rang. 'Excuse me for a second, Ron – probably the new goddamn night editor. Feel like a fucking nursemaid sometimes.' But it wasn't Merle Sanger.

'You having a nice night, Mr Donovan?' The voice was strangely robotic, as if it had been electronically distorted.

'Sorry, who is this?'

'Listen very closely Mr Donovan. Do exactly as I say.'

'Excuse me, who the hell are you?'

'There's an envelope for you at reception. Pick it up. And I'll call you back in five minutes. But don't tell your fat friend sitting on the deck. Do it, check the contents in private, and return as if nothing has happened.'

Ron smiled back at Harry and he forced a strained return grin.

'Well, what are you waiting for?' Then the line went dead.

'I'm sorry, Ron . . . I'll be back in five minutes.'

'Anything wrong?'

'Newsroom politics. I'll be back in a moment.'

'Apparently you have something for me. Name's Harry Donovan.'

The young Hispanic woman on reception rifled in a bottom drawer and pulled out a white manila envelope.

'This what you're looking for?' she said.

'When was this delivered?'

'I believe it was delivered by hand earlier today.'

'What did the guy look like?'

'I'm sorry, sir, I have no idea. Just started my night shift.'

'Thanks.'

'Enjoy the rest of your night, sir.'

Harry headed into a restroom next to reception and ripped open the envelope. Inside were some close-up pictures of him and Andrew on Crandon Beach.

He took a few moments to compose himself. Then he placed the photos and the envelope in an inside pocket of his jacket and returned to the deck.

'Everything okay?' Ron asked.

'Maybe it's time I looked for another job,' Harry said ruefully, picking up his Scotch.

'Same old shit,' said Ron, gazing off into the darkness.

Harry's phone rang again. 'Are you sitting comfortably, Harry?' said the voice.

'I'm sorry, Ron – no rest for the wicked. Can you excuse me?'

'I'll be thinking in a moment that you're having an affair.' Ron patted his friend on the shoulder, then tapped the side of his glass. 'Need a refill anyway. Same again?'

'Thanks.'

Ron weaved his way to the bar.

'Okay, talk,' said Harry.

'All men have secrets, they say. Some darker than others. And I appreciate why you wouldn't want your friends or colleagues to know what I know. The problem is that when people like me come calling, it makes men with secrets more vulnerable.'

'What the hell is that supposed to mean?'

'I assume that, as executive editor of the *Herald*, you heard about that tragic incident – body found in the Everglades?'

'Look, I don't know who you are or what—'

'Call off the investigation.'

'What?'

'Don't be a dumbass, Harry. Deborah Jones, your lovely investigations editor, was given the go-ahead by Sam Goldberg to look into this. She's sniffing around. And we don't want that. Is that clear enough?'

'Truly, I have no idea what you are talking about, and that's the truth.'

'Then you're being kept out of the loop.'

Harry felt himself go hot. 'Listen, even if there is an

investigation underway, I can't order it to be halted just because—'

'You're not listening to me, Harry. The investigation is causing the people I work for great displeasure. It needs to stop. Pull the plug. Now. Or else.'

'Or else what?'

A long silence elapsed. 'Your wife doesn't know about Andrew, does she, Harry? Or that one-night stand with your PA, Rebecca Sinez?'

'I think we've talked long enough. I'm going to turn this matter over to the police.'

'I'd think long and hard if I were you. The fancy house on Key Biscayne your wife – the heiress to an eighty-million-dollar real-estate fortune – owns. You wanna give all that up? I mean, do you really?'

Harry said nothing.

'I seem to have got your attention at last.'

'I will not be blackmailed, do you hear me?'

'You're not listening to me, Harry. You've got to make the right call. Or else this carefully constructed and ordered life that you have will disintegrate before your very eyes.'

12

Deborah took her laptop over to the kitchen table and logged onto the MIT website, checking out the computer faculty. Over the course of the morning, over numerous coffees, she put in calls to everyone and anyone. She started at the top of the list with the director – Professor Jon Weitners – then worked her way down.

It was mind-boggling what they did there. Engineering technology based on biology, computer networks and data communication, algorithms for network application, the theory of parallel computing, intelligent interfaces and pattern languages for automated text-editing, genetic programming, sensor networks, quantum computing, real-time-oriented compiler technology.

By mid-afternoon Deborah had exhausted all avenues there and was frustrated that no one had called her back. Then she remembered that John Hudson had mentioned the phrase 'social engineering'. What did that mean, exactly? She decided to ask the *Miami Herald*'s own Marco Martinez whose specialty was technology issues. Sounding like a jaded teacher, he explained the term to her.

'Everyone who uses a computer knows about fire-walls, anti-virus software, all that stuff, right?'

'I guess so.'

'It's designed to safeguard the computer or a computer network from attack from hackers, benign or malevolent. The basic aim of social engineering is the same as hacking, i.e. network intrusion, espionage, identity theft, whatever. You with me?'

'So far.'

'It's really all about gaining unauthorized access from a person to information, be it files, passwords, e-mails, whatever, rather than breaking into a system. By imper-sonating someone, you can convince another person to disclose confidential information, like a password. Then there's "dumpster diving", some call it "trashing", where information can be gained through potential security leaks in company trash. Printouts of passwords, source codes, memos. All these things can be exploited by social-engineering hackers. They will call up a help desk and pretend they're from a phone company. There was one case where some hacker called up and said, "Hey, I'm from AT&T, I'm stuck on a pole. You mind punching in a few buttons for me?" He got straight into the company's files.'

Marco was getting into his stride now.

'You know a real favorite? Stealing the cellphone of a relative. Maybe a sister or brother or mother or wife of the target. If you're smart enough, you can send a text message to the hack's BlackBerry. Because the number of the relative is not viewed as a threat, the target opens the message and so activates a virus, perhaps a Trojan. So a remote user can then gain access to the target's files. Once again, it is all about trust.'

'I feel like I'm living in the dark ages, Marco.'

He laughed. 'Social-engineering attacks take time, perhaps days, sometimes weeks, tracking movements. A stolen smartphone can do all sorts of damage.'

Flamingo Park's twenty-five-yard heated outdoor pool was empty as Deborah did some front-crawl power laps at the end of a frustrating day. She felt her shoulders finally begin to relax as she swam hard. The broiling sun was low in the sky. Nearby the sound of innocent laughter bubbled up from children as they played on the water slides, blissfully unaware that only yards from the children's playpool Jenny Forbes – a brilliant Miami lawyer – had been raped and left for dead twenty years ago. It was also the place where her grandfather had exacted his revenge on Joe O'Neill.

Deborah tried not to think about it. Instead, she focused on whether anyone at MIT would return her calls. On and on she swam, clocking up the laps.

She felt herself shutting off. Physical activity, whether it was swimming, soccer or jogging, was the only way she had of coping with the stresses of her job. As she neared her thirtieth lap she felt the endorphins kick in, flooding her body. She powered on for another twenty, her heart now racing, feeling stronger and sharper.

Afterwards, during the short walk back to her apartment, sports bag slung over her shoulder, her cellphone rang.

'Miss Jones?' It was a woman's voice.

'Yes.'

'Good evening, Miss Jones. Professor Levin. I'm senior research professor with MIT's Computer Science and Artificial Intelligence Laboratory. You called about John Hudson.'

13

'Thank you so much, Professor, for getting back to me. I guess you must all be very busy, since you are the only person so far to return my call.'

'Around eleven this morning, the director of the lab called us all together and instructed us not to speak to the media about this. We are not even supposed to confirm that John was a student here. But I for one will not remain silent.'

'I'm grateful for that. Did you know John Hudson well?'

'He was, quite simply, the most brilliant student I've ever worked with.'

'Tell me more about him. And I don't mean necessarily what his parents want to hear.'

'Like I said, he was really smart, with a great future ahead of him. But his attendance record was terrible. The students who make it to MIT are the brightest of the bright, and we expect nothing but the best from them. But I think John had a real problem with authority. I gather he had got into hacking in a big way. Apparently he was obsessed with finding out about the twenty-eight censored pages in the Congressional Inquiry Report on the September 11 attacks. Does that mean anything to you?'

'You mean the pages which were blanked out of the published report because they could be embarrassing for a foreign government – Saudi Arabia, wasn't it? And because of our links to that regime?'

'Exactly. The White House didn't want us to know. John, like many of us, felt the report should be published in full.'

'You think he might have hacked into a government computer to find out?'

'Apparently, John was developing his own programs. He was part of an organization called the Cult of the Dead Cow – an elite group of hackers.'

Holding the phone tight to her ear as traffic roared past, Deborah stood in the shade of some huge palms on Meridian Avenue.

'He was also very interested in wireless free data communication. Through these Bluetooth-configured smartphones. I gather John had been spending a lot of time developing Trojan viruses. Your anti-virus program on your computer sweeps for them while you're online. But smartphones are just as susceptible to hacking. It is technically possible for the data on a mobile phone which has been hacked to be cleaned out of the phone's memory. Sensitive files, you name it.'

'Can you explain in layman's terms what exactly a Trojan virus does?'

'Basically, it allows a remote user a means of gaining access to a victim's machine without their knowledge. Then the user is free to browse the files to see if there's anything they want. John Hudson was in a league of his own.'

'Do you think John was the sort of person who would want to end his life?' Deborah asked.

'Never in a million years. He was outgoing; he was funny.'

'Was there a girl?'

'I don't know.'

'Do you think his hacking could've gotten him killed?'

'Maybe. John Hudson was a remarkable young man. But he had one fatal weakness. He was an idealist.'

Deborah shielded her eyes from the shafts of sunlight piercing the palm leaves. 'And that's a weakness?'

'Miss Jones, I'm a throwback to the 1960s. Part of the Woodstock generation. His mindset was very similar to mine. He believed in the people, and he believed in the truth. And, in my view quite correctly, he didn't trust our government. There was someone he did trust, however. A guy by the name of Richard Turner. Does that name mean anything to you, Miss Jones?'

Deborah unzipped the side pocket of her sports bag for the pen and small notepad she kept there. Then she wrote the name down, underlining it twice. 'No – should it?'

'Richard was an MIT dropout from the 1960s. Well known among the hacking fraternity. Made a big name for himself in the 1980s.'

'What was so special about him?'

'According to folklore, he hacked the Pentagon, NASA, NSA and the CIA, all using his own programs. He'd served time for anti-Vietnam protests, and I'm led to believe he now lives a quiet life in New York. You should try and talk to him about John Hudson.'

'You've been most helpful, Professor, and very courageous. I appreciate your candor.'

'Look, I've gotta go. We've got a faculty dinner in about an hour.'

'Professor, I owe you one.'

14

The freezing-cold air of New York was a shock to Nathan's system which was more attuned to the warmer climes of Florida. He could see his breath as he walked around the East Village trying to pass the time – and trying to keep warm – while waiting on the call. He was smoking a cigarette, collar upturned against the biting wind, as he headed along East Third Street, reacquainting himself with the old neighborhood.

He passed the Hell's Angel HQ in Manhattan, stealing a quick glance at a couple of longhairs on big Harleys outside. Nothing seemed to have changed there. They stared at him as he walked on, wondering if he was a cop. He couldn't abide those long-haired fuckers. Most were angel-dust dealers or just plain badass bikers looking for a fight. He'd have been delighted to oblige. It wouldn't have been the first time he'd smashed a pool cue into some moron's face. But their clubhouse was under surveillance and he had no wish to draw attention to himself.

The cameras were situated high up beside a fire escape, strafing the area for cops or for other biker gangs trying to hassle Angels heading in or out.

Nathan wandered over to Broadway, then crossed Fourth Avenue at Astor Place. In St Mark's Place he stopped beside a basement stairway to light up another cigarette.

All around, every variation of decadent western culture was on show. Leather freaks, crew-cut lesbians, black bikers, punks, old hippies, skateboard kids smoking weed. And the razor-wire fences and gang graffiti scrawled on down-at-heel stores.

When Nathan had been growing up, anything between 14th Street and Houston was the Lower East Side. Now most people called it the East Village – anything to link it with the more affluent bohemia of Greenwich Village.

It had started with the developers in the 1980s. Junkies, welfare mothers, gangs and penniless artists had populated the high-crime slum area where he grew up. But now it had become a lot more commercial. The sidewalks were cleaner, there was less graffiti. Now Japanese, Indian and Ukrainian restaurants sat side by side with bondage stores, vintage boutiques, art galleries and secondhand music shops, although there was still a hint of danger in the air.

Nathan remembered walking the same streets as a

boy in the early-to-mid-1970s with an empty belly and an aching heart, relying on church handouts of free soup and old clothes as the city headed for bankruptcy, crime out of control, burned-out buildings on every street. He looked after his younger sister the best he could.

Begging for dimes from strangers, hanging around outside bars and dives, hands cupped, wanting some 'bread'. He meant both money and food. He didn't starve. And neither did his sister.

No thanks to their father, who seemed to spend most of his days in a flophouse on the Bowery.

He remembered walking the streets hand in hand with his sister, wearing strange clothes, the hippies laughing at them, asking if he wanted a smoke. He told them no and was embarrassed, which made them laugh even more.

He also remembered, as a teenager, having to learn to fight to stay alive as he walked home from Seward Park High School on Grand Street. His sister, who surfed the Net these days, told him that it was now called the Lower Manhattan Arts Academy.

Nathan stole a glance down the stairs at a basement on St Mark's. The drapes were drawn but there was a light on inside. The subject was at home, only yards from where Nathan stood. He looked around, getting his bearings again after all this time.

Everything seemed smaller. Kids were walking around yapping into cellphones, unheard of in his days.

Nathan took one final look down the basement steps

and glanced at his watch. Then he pulled out his own cellphone. He needed to find out what was going on.

'Hey, Nath, how goes it?'

'I'm in position. Awaiting instruction.'

A long pause before the handler spoke. 'Do not enter the building at this moment. But if he makes a move, then it's game on.'

Nathan dropped his cigarette, grinding it out with the heel of his boot. 'Affirmative.'

There was a café nearby and he took a window seat with a bird's-eye view of the basement entrance.

This was the part that Nathan hated the most. The hanging around, trying to kill time.

He popped a couple of steroid pills and washed them down with a strong coffee. Now Nathan was ready for anything.

15

There were mentions of Richard Turner in countless chat rooms, message boards and articles on the Internet, and one essay by a computer software engineer dubbing him the 'Godfather of Hackers'. But Deborah drew a blank on how to locate him.

She called Sam.

'I was speaking to one of John Hudson's professors at MIT about an hour ago. She was quite helpful. I need to track down a guy called Richard Turner.'

'You tried Nexus?'

'Of course.'

'What about Larry Coen? He knows everybody.'

'He's on vacation this week.'

'So he is.'

'All I know is this guy's supposed to be in New York.'

'You don't fly as a rule, do you, Deborah?'

'I'll make an exception in this case.'

'Okay, you're in business.'

'You mentioned about an old friend of yours from way back. Thomas McNally.'

'It'll cost the paper serious money.'

'So, are you going to help me or not?'

An hour later, Deborah arrived at the Bank of America Tower in downtown Miami – the third-largest skyscraper in the city. It was home to some of the country's most powerful firms and government agencies. Global investment banks, high-powered legal firms, management consultants, private-equity companies and various government bodies. McNally had a large office on the twenty-first floor – but his firm was not listed in the tenant directory, nor in the phone directory for that matter.

Thomas 'Tequila' McNally had previously worked as a special agent in the FBI's Miami office, eventually heading up the bureau. But his gambling debts and drinking binges hadn't gone down too well with his superiors, and he'd been forced to resign.

He set up a small firm of private investigators, Information Inc., which was widely used by big American corporations to do background checks on employees. They dug up address histories, phone numbers, possible aliases, neighbors, criminal and civil records checks, and marriage records. Not to mention doing searches of utility company records, court records, county records, property records, business records and more. Hard-to-get addresses were McNally's specialty.

He didn't advertise, and all his clients came to him because he'd been recommended to them by satisfied customers.

Deborah felt nervous as she rode the elevator to the eleventh-floor Sky Lobby Terrace within the tower, wondering if McNally would turn up at such short notice. She stepped out onto the balmy candlelit terrace that was bedecked in marble and gold. Dozens of people dined alfresco by a reflecting pool, the night lights of the city all around.

The smell of chargrilled steaks and hot spices mingled with cigarette smoke in the dark, humid Miami air.

'Miss Jones, I presume.'

Deborah turned round and saw a large avuncular man wearing a Panama hat and a creased cream linen suit. 'You must be—'

'Let's take a seat, and we can shoot the breeze.'

Deborah followed him to a reserved table where an ice bucket and a bottle of champagne were ready for them. They sat down.

'I'm afraid I haven't got too much time this evening, Miss Jones.'

A waiter appeared and McNally nodded to him. The bottle of champagne was uncorked and two flutes poured. Deborah didn't mention that she didn't drink.

'You got a name?' he asked.

'Richard Turner. He could be in New York. He studied at MIT. That's about it . . .'

McNally knocked back his glass of champagne in a

couple of gulps. 'You mind telling me what you're investigating?'

Deborah took a few seconds before she answered. 'We're looking into the death of Bill Hudson's son John.'

'I read about that.' McNally poured himself another glass. 'So, how long you worked for Sam?'

'A few years.'

'I believe you and him are an item – is that right?'

Deborah just smiled.

'He's a good man.' McNally savored the next long sip of Piper-Heidsieck. 'How are Richard Turner and John Hudson linked?'

'I believe both of them were hackers.'

'Interesting.'

'John Hudson tried to contact me with a story, after hacking into someone's computer or smartphone.'

'And you think this Richard Turner might be able to help you?'

'I don't have any other leads,' Deborah said.

McNally looked out over the bright lights of the city at night. 'Miami's the future. A twenty-first-century city. And there's big money to be made here. Big opportunities for those who know how to take them. It's like the new frontier. Condos flying up everywhere. Anything's possible. But what most people don't realize is that rules don't mean shit down here. Colombian drug gangs are crazy. Would shoot their own mother if she threatened their turf. Politicians, cops, everyone is taking a slice of the pie. Even the Miami property bubble bursting is not putting off the developers, buying up land like there's no tomorrow. Yeah, this is the place to be now. And believe me, Florida's a big, big place, and it's easy to disappear, if you know what I mean.'

'I don't follow.'

'Look, I'll do my best to find this guy. But what I can tell you for nothing is that when the son of a top Miami lawyer winds up dead in the Everglades, with no witnesses, you know you're dealing with serious people. You need to know this before you go any further. Has it occurred to you that this guy may not want to be found?'

'Of course. That's why I've come to you.'

McNally stared off into the distance. 'Okay. Leave it with me.'

16

By the time Deborah got home there was a message on her BlackBerry and an address in Lower Manhattan. Then she called Sam.

His last words echoed in her ear as her cab snaked through traffic on the way to Miami International Airport: 'Be smart, and take care.'

Deborah caught the last flight of the evening out of Miami, her first time in the air for more than five years. She hadn't flown since her rape-induced breakdown had made her terrified of taking a plane. It was a nail-biting three hours – eyes closed, gripping the armrests of her seat.

Just before midnight, with the New York air bitterly cold after the warmth of Florida, Deborah hailed a taxi outside JFK.

Her heart started pumping hard as the cab crossed the Williamsburg Bridge, the dark waters of the East River glittering below.

Deborah looked out at the ethnic restaurants of Lower Manhattan, street vendors, newsstands, steam rising out of manhole covers.

The cab pulled up outside a Japanese noodle bar. The sidewalk, despite the hour, was teeming with people. 'This looks like it,' the driver said.

Above the restaurant was a punk-rock clothing and accessories store – Search and Destroy. Thrash metal blared out from a window.

Deborah paid the driver before stepping out onto the sidewalk. The smell of steamed rice, spicy meats and smoke hit her full on.

She walked gingerly for fifty yards along the cracked icy sidewalk and then spotted the number painted on steel steps that led down to a dark basement.

Deborah took a deep breath and opened the wrought-iron gate. The steps were slippery and she gripped the handrail tight. She pressed the buzzer and held it down for a couple of seconds. 'Come on, come on,' she muttered, stamping her feet.

Bars on the window, curtains shut tight.

She tried again but there was no reply.

Deborah knocked on the door. Rat-a-tat-tat. And then again.

'You ain't gonna find nobody there.' Staring down at Deborah from street level was a young black woman wearing tight jeans and a skimpy top, hugging herself to keep warm while smoking a cigarette.

'I'm sorry?'

'I said you ain't gonna find nobody there.'

'Do you know who lives here?'

'Sure I do.'

Deborah said nothing, wondering if the young woman was for real.

'You IRS?'

'I'm a reporter. I need to speak to Richard Turner.'

The woman laughed, showing some gold in her teeth. 'You know what time it is, honey?'

'Yeah, I know it's late.'

'Well, he ain't home. That boy is always on the move. Know what I'm saying?'

Deborah climbed the steps back up to the street level. 'You seem to know Richard quite well.'

'I know everyone around here. I know the freaks, the punk kids, the brothers, the Japanese, Bangladeshis, I know what's going on, y'understand?'

'Do you know where I can find him?'

The young woman just shrugged.

Deborah opened her wallet and took out a crisp one hundred dollar bill. 'Can you help me?'

The young woman tried to grab the money but Deborah was too quick for her.

'I need an address. I was told that Richard lived here.'

'He does live here. At least, some of the time. The place belongs to an old friend of his.'

Deborah shrugged.

'Abbie Hoffman and his wife lived here, way back in the 1960s.'

Deborah knew that the woman was referring to one of America's most vocal anti-Vietnam activists, and leader of the Yippies – the Youth International Party.

The young woman eyed the note in Deborah's grip. 'Richard's like me. He preferred the East Village when it was rough and ready. Before the developers and the yuppies moved in. Can hardly afford to live in this goddamn city anymore.'

Deborah gave her the money. She gazed at it for a few seconds, as if checking to see if the note was a fake, before she looked again at Deborah, her eyes watery. 'You might wanna head across to Brooklyn. I know Richard sometimes likes to spend a night or two at a time over there, when he feels the heat's on.'

'I need an address.'

'Down by the waterfront.'

'Can you be a little more precise?'

'Imlay Street. 160 Imlay Street. You should catch him there.'

'What does he look like, just so I know?'

'Always wears a red bandana and sneakers, long hair. Think he's still going through a Bruce Springsteen thing.' She gave a wistful smile. 'Shit. Richard's just a kid at heart. But don't tell him I told you so, okay?'

The woman turned on her heel and headed towards a bar nearly a block away.

All of a sudden Deborah's cellphone rang.

'Just calling to see you arrived safely.' Sam's reassuring voice sent a warm glow through her body.

'I'm fine. But McNally only gave me one address. I need to check out Turner tomorrow morning in Brooklyn.'

'Sorry, Debs. You're wanted back in Miami by the big chief.'

'Donovan?'

'He wants you here for ten o'clock.'

'But that's not possible, Sam. You know that.'

Sam sighed. 'He's talking about launching another investigation into the Scott Carver debacle. And he's not in the mood for any excuses. He wants you on the first flight tomorrow morning. It gets into Miami just before nine, which'll give you time to get some shut-eye and be in his office for ten.'

'So I've come all this way for nothing.'

'If you don't make the red-eye, then even I won't be able to pull any strings for you. Am I making myself clear?'

'I don't believe what I'm hearing.'

'No arguments, Deborah. I'll see you tomorrow.'

Deborah didn't reply.

'You're pissed at me, aren't you?' Sam asked. 'I don't blame you.'

'Oh, Sam.' Deborah kicked an empty Coke can lying on the sidewalk onto the road. 'Goddamn it,' she muttered.

Then she spotted a cab.

★　★　★

The dark narrow cobbled streets of Brooklyn's southern waterfront – the run-down industrial enclave of Red Hook – were a world away from Manhattan.

Deborah cursed her impetuousness as the cab hurtled down deserted streets. Behind the buildings the silhouettes of old cranes loomed large in the freezing night. This had once been the heart of blue-collar New York. Longshoremen, truckers, scrapyards. The film *On the Waterfront* only helped to enhance its tough reputation – corrupt unions, violent clashes with bosses, the mob in the background. But those days were long gone.

Now, in the early hours of the morning, the only person around was an old black man, wrapped in blankets and making his way slowly down the dimly lit street, occasionally slugging from a bottle in a brown paper bag.

The driver pulled up outside a huge six-storey industrial building that was covered in black construction netting. He pointed to a door with the number 160 daubed on it in white paint.

'You sure this is where you want to go, lady?'

'No, I'm not.'

The driver turned round. 'So, you getting out here or not? I've got a wife and two kids to feed, you understand?'

Deborah checked the meter and handed him fifty dollars, opening her door.

'You want me to hang around?' the driver asked. 'It'll cost you another fifty, though. And the same again to get you back into Manhattan.'

78

'How much to JFK?'

'That'll be fifty dollars as well.'

'That's fine. Wait here.'

'Look, you *sure* this is the right address? Doesn't look like anyone's home.'

'I won't be long.' Deborah's stomach knotted as she stepped out of the cab. A metal sign for the building company carrying out the renovations rattled against the scaffolding.

The warehouse door was partially concealed by the black netting. She pushed it open, edging her way into the pitch darkness. The netting caught in her hair like a thick spider's web and she had to shake herself clear.

Leaving the door ajar to let light in from the street, Deborah waited for her eyes to adjust to the blackness. The place smelled of damp wood and piss.

'I'm looking for Richard Turner!' she shouted, feeling faintly ridiculous. Her voice echoed around the old stone walls and the wooden beams.

Pale moonlight seeped in through the windows. On the ground, a couple of yards away to her right, she spotted what looked like a used condom and a blood-smeared syringe. Against her better judgment she walked in, treading very carefully on the old wooden floors, glad that she was wearing a sturdy pair of Timberlands.

Up ahead she could just make out some dusty wooden stairs and she headed slowly towards them.

Red eyes were staring at her.

Deborah froze. It was a rat. She stamped her foot and

the rodent scurried off into the darkness. To her right, through the shattered panes of the windows, the cold night air blasted in. She could make out the Statue of Liberty and the reassuring Manhattan skyline, its warm lights twinkling in the distance. That's where I should be, she thought, snuggled up in a nice hotel, not scouring some run-down old squat for a washed-out hippie.

It was crazy. Her heart was racing as she looked up at the huge dark space at the top of the stairs.

Was he up there?

Deborah took the first step. And then the second. Higher and higher, climbing up to the first floor of the old warehouse, guided only by the faint light.

At the top of the stairs she stopped as she spotted something on the ground. It was the tail end of a reefer.

An archway led through to another cavernous room, even darker, its window space boarded up. She walked a few steps and stopped, her nose wrinkling at the stench of urine and excrement.

Why on earth would Richard Turner use such a place when he had a basement apartment in the East Village?

There was a noise from upstairs. Deborah stopped dead and listened. It was rock music, playing low. Resisting the inner voice that was telling her to get out of there, she advanced up the next flight of stairs.

She recognized the song. 'Keep on Chooglin'' by Creedence Clearwater Revival. She remembered it from seeing John Fogerty in concert in San Francisco with Brett, in her first year at Berkeley.

There was a whiff of old cigarettes and stale beer. Deborah detected the distinctive sickly-sweet smell of hash.

'Richard?' she said querulously, eyes screwed up in the gloom. She could vaguely make out what looked like an old mattress and a couple of beer cans.

Her leg banged against something on the ground and she tripped and fell over, banging her head painfully on the floor. 'Goddamn!' she muttered as her hand went up to touch where it hurt. She felt warm blood.

Deborah wiped her hands on her jeans.

There was a silvery glint on the floor beside her. It was a metallic lighter, with 'RT' inscribed on it. She flicked it on and the light revealed a cavernous space.

John Fogerty's rasping vocals and twangy guitar filled the fetid air. In the flickering glow of the lighter she could see a man's body, hanging by a thick brown leather belt. A red bandana covered his eyes.

17

The sun streamed through the blinds of the conference room when Sam walked in just before eight, drinking a coffee and holding that morning's *Herald*. He felt emotionally drained through worry and lack of sleep.

Harry Donovan, the paper's Executive Editor, was already there, sitting grim-faced at one end of the huge polished table. Papers and documents were spread out.

Sam took off his jacket and sat down, placing his coffee and the newspaper on the table. 'You manage to get in touch with our esteemed publisher yet?' He was referring to Juan Garcia who was still trekking in the Andes.

Harry nodded and put on his glasses. 'What's the latest on Deborah?'

'Fine. She was a little shaken up, as you can imagine, but she's okay. We've got a lawyer with her.'

'Is she still in New York?'

'She was just over an hour ago. She's hoping to fly back this afternoon.'

Harry cleared his throat. 'Sam, firstly I'd like to say I'm glad Deborah is safe and well. Must've been a helluva shock.'

Sam smiled.

'But I am, to put it mildly, mighty pissed off that I was kept in the dark about this.'

'It was very last-minute.'

'Listen to me, Sam, and listen good. I have got a right to know what is happening on this paper, any developments on any story, any time, day or night. Do you understand me?'

'Of course. But things can happen – you know the drill.'

'Don't fuck with me, Sam. I mean, what the hell was Deborah doing in Brooklyn in the middle of the night?'

'Chasing down a lead. That's what we do.'

Harry leaned back in his seat. 'I don't like to be made to look a fool. This happens again and we're going to be having some serious words. You hear what I'm saying?'

'Loud and clear.'

'Okay. In future, even if it's only an e-mail I want to know what is going on with our journalists. At all times. You understand?'

Sam nodded but said nothing.

Harry sighed. 'And yeah, I managed to get hold of Juan.'

'What did he have to say for himself?'

'Would it surprise you to hear that he already knew? Apparently he received a call to his cellphone around five a.m. Eastern Time, from Hablo.' He was referring to the editor of *El Nuevo*, the *Herald*'s Spanish-language paper on the sixth floor.

'Bullshit.'

'Now, I know you and Hablo don't see eye to eye on many things,' Harry said. 'But hear me out. Hablo was the initial contact. He was woken by a long-time source around half past four this morning, to do with some big story about pro-Castro spies operating in Little Havana. But then this source goes on to mention how a *Miami Herald* journalist had just found a body in Brooklyn.'

'Did he reveal the name of this source, or do we have to take it on trust?'

'If you let me finish, Sam. Juan spoke to the source himself. And he turns out to be one of the most powerful men in the intelligence community. It looks as though Deborah may have inadvertently jeopardized a major investigation they were working on. National security—'

'Sorry to interrupt, but who is this guy?'

'He didn't say.'

'Juan didn't confide in the Executive Editor of the *Miami Herald* the identity of this source? Come on, Harry.'

'Basically, we are being asked to halt Deborah's inquiries until their own investigation is concluded.'

'You've got to be kidding.'

'I've spoken to Juan and we both feel that it would be best for all if—'

'So what happened to our reputation for fearless journalism?'

'We've got responsibilities as well.'

'You're not buying that crock of shit, are you?'

'For the time being – yes. Look, Sam, I give you absolute freedom, and Juan gives me free rein as well. Now, I have backed you on every story we've printed, no matter the flak – am I right?'

Sam nodded but stayed quiet.

'The way I see it, we have a college kid – whose father is a friend of yours – who winds up dead. It's tragic, but would it be too much to surmise that he might've taken an airboat for a midnight jaunt across the Everglades and it all went horribly wrong? Secondly, we have some old Sixties hippie, who may or may not be a hacker, who looks like he's hanged himself.'

'Who could be involved—'

'Sam, whilst I'm very sad for the loss of your friend's son—'

'How long has Juan been with us? Six, seven months? All he knows is provincial newspapers. He's out of his depth.'

'He was headhunted quite specifically.'

'He's a fucking accountant. He doesn't know news from shit.'

'Juan Garcia is one of the top publishers in America.'

Sam could feel his blood boiling. 'Hablo has never forgiven me for outing his ties with the CIA, has he? That's what all this comes down to, isn't it?'

'This isn't personal, Sam. And don't for one minute think it is.'

But Sam knew that it was. Several years earlier the *Miami Herald* had revealed that three *El Nuevo* journalists – two staffers and a freelancer – were being paid by the American government to air anti-Castro propaganda. The journalists had been fired, but after a backlash from the Cuban community they were reinstated. It transpired later that the journalists had in fact been given the go-ahead by a former editor of *El Nuevo*, Ramon Munoz, to work for TV Marti and Radio Marti which had been founded by the American government as part of the US war of attrition against Castro. Sam had been outraged and had not hidden the fact.

'So are you telling me to tell Deborah that her investigation is over?'

'You got it in one, Sam.'

Sam stormed out of the conference room and straight up to the sixth floor. Hablo was sitting in his office reading his paper, his feet on his desk.

'You mind telling me why you didn't feel the need to speak to me first?' Sam snapped.

'About what?'

'About this so-called intelligence source asking us to get Deborah to lay off.'

Hablo gave a tight smile. 'He wanted to speak to Juan confidentially.'

'So who is this source of yours? I'd like to speak to him.'

'I'm sorry, Sam, you know that's not possible.'

'You haven't heard the last of this,' Sam said and slammed the door behind him as he stormed out.

He mulled things over for the next hour. Then he headed out to the airport to pick up Deborah. She looked tired and drawn.

Sam hugged her tight and quickly relayed the conversation with Donovan. 'Here's the plan,' he said. 'I want the investigation to continue. Work from home. But not even Harry Donovan gets to know about this. Do you understand?'

18

It was dark when Harry Donovan sped across the Rickenbacker causeway and back to his sprawling waterfront home on South Mashta Drive, Key Biscayne. He poured himself a large Scotch and switched on CNN on the huge plasma TV. But he wasn't in the mood for apocalyptic stories about famines and floods and bombings.

He switched the set off and stared out of the floor-to-ceiling windows across the bay towards the dazzling skyline of Miami. It had been a hell of a day.

Harry couldn't concentrate on his work. He felt sick at the prospect of his comfortable existence being turned upside down. A twenty-year marriage to his pushy and fabulously wealthy real-estate heiress wife Jacqueline Simpson, his millionaire lifestyle and their great homes, would all be jeopardized. As would his job at the *Herald* – Jacqueline's family's large shareholding in the paper's parent company would see to that. Only the unexpected intervention of Juan Garcia was in his favor.

The phone rang and he jumped.

'Listen to this, Harry,' his wife said breathlessly. 'You are not going to believe who's staying in the next suite to me at the Carlyle!'

'I don't know . . . George Clooney?'

'The British Foreign Secretary. He's asked me to join him for dinner this evening.'

'That's terrific, honey,' Harry said, feigning interest.

'So, what kind of day have you had, Harry?'

'Hectic.'

'Have you eaten yet?'

'I can fix myself a sandwich later. I managed lunch with the mayor, so I'm not hungry.'

'Oh.' Jacqueline was a world-class networker. 'How is he? Hope you apologized for the canapés we served last time? The caviar wasn't even beluga. What's he going to think?'

'Diaz took it all in his stride as he always does. He wouldn't know beluga from Belgium.'

'Did you tell him I fired the caterer?'

'Sure. Look, darling, I've got a stack of paperwork to finish – do you mind if I call you tomorrow morning?'

'You can catch me at the hotel until noon if you need me, then I'll be off to the airport. See you tomorrow night. Love you.'

'Love you too, honey.'

Harry hung up and finished his drink. He paced up

and down, his footsteps on the marble floor echoing around the huge cathedral ceilings. He felt as if he was going out of his mind. He needed to talk to Rebecca. He phoned her. But it was his son who answered.

'Hey, Andrew, how was school today?'

'Gimme a break, Dad. Calculus.'

Harry groaned.

'It wasn't so bad. Mr Laursen took us kayaking out on the bay this afternoon.'

'Andrew, can you put your mother on?'

'Sure, Dad. See you at the weekend.'

A few moments later, his former PA came on the line. 'Harry, what a lovely surprise.'

'Rebecca, we need to talk.'

'Now?'

'Right now. Face to face.'

'Are you okay, Harry?'

'Fifteen minutes – okay?'

'I'll put the coffee on.'

Rebecca was wearing that great perfume again when he arrived at the nearby third-floor two-bedroom condo on Ocean Park Drive that he'd found for them. She pecked him on the cheek and drew him quickly inside. Andrew gave him a high five and they made small talk about his school for a few minutes before Harry was shown into the kitchen.

'So,' Rebecca said, handing him a mug of strong coffee, 'what's the big hurry? You decided to leave your wife at long last?'

Harry felt his cheeks flush. 'Not quite. Something a bit more . . . delicate.'

Rebecca shrugged.

Reaching into his pocket, Harry brought out the pictures taken on Crandon Beach.

Rebecca shut the kitchen door for privacy. 'What the hell is going on?'

'I'm being blackmailed to stop a bona fide investigation into suspicious deaths. We need to go to the cops. I just wanted you to know where we stand before I make the call.'

Rebecca bit her lower lip. 'Hang on a minute, Harry. If you go to the cops you risk everything. Jacqueline will freak out. Then she'll divorce you, and probably enforce the pre-nup.'

'I'm not interested in her money.'

'I don't have that luxury. We've got to think of Andrew. My salary at the Ritz-Carlton might be okay, but it's not enough to pay for this place.'

'I can take care of everything.'

'Harry, we both know that it's her money that really pays for this condo, her money that pays for Andrew's school fees, her money that allows us to take nice vacations.'

'Look, as it stands, I've managed to get the investigation put on hold. But we can't allow this creep to get away with this.'

'Wouldn't it be smarter to let this blow over?'

'Rebecca, I can't believe what you're saying. We need to bite the bullet here.'

'So you'll lose your job, you'll be thrown out of that fancy waterfront house, we might lose this place. Do you really want to risk all that? You might not find another job for months, maybe more. What do we do in the meantime? Pray?'

'I have savings. Investments.'

'Gimme a break. Harry, the investigation's over. You said so yourself. What have you got to worry about?'

'My conscience.'

'Just think for a moment. How do you think the kids at school are going to react when our story is plastered all over the papers? Reporters will be camped outside the gatehouse. I don't want that. Do you? The police will call all their favorite crime reporters with the full gory details.'

'I know some people. Not cops, but people that could help us.'

'Who?'

'Feds, amongst others. If I speak to them, hopefully they'll agree to handle this discreetly.'

Rebecca ran a hand through her long luscious chestnut-brown hair. 'And if they don't?'

'I think we need to be strong. I think it's time to call this guy's bluff.'

'Call his bluff? You cannot be serious! You'd destroy everything we have.'

'So what do you suggest in the meantime?'

'Trust me. It'll blow over. You'll see.'

19

The following night, under the harsh floodlights of Palmer Park, Deborah and the rest of the girls from the Overtown Women's Soccer Team were running energy-sapping laps on the rock-hard ground. The team, made up mostly of former vice girls, junkies and other hard-luck stories who hailed from Miami's impoverished black inner city, had acted as a focal point for the women concerned since the club had been formed five years earlier.

'I don't think I've ever seen such a sad-looking group of fat-assed women in all my goddamn life,' Faith shouted from the sidelines. 'What the hell is the matter with you? Pick it up, girls, and show old Faith that you ain't just killing time. I want you to suck up all the pain – and that includes you, Deborah Jones. Don't think I don't notice you slacking. Come on, now – let's get it going.'

Deborah felt every muscle tighten as the session wore on. The sweat poured off her. But it was good to be out training with the girls, listening to them moaning about boyfriends and husbands, cursing their children and generally bad-mouthing anybody within earshot.

She knew how each and every one of them had dug deep, determined to show their kids that there was a better way – that a world existed that wasn't about dealing drugs or selling your body but which involved self-respect, sacrifice and hard work.

The problem was that a large number of the children were stuck in underachieving schools, with little realistic chance of getting into good colleges unless they won a rare sports scholarship. Deborah had managed to persuade Sam to take on a smart eighteen-year-old boy, Martin Blackwell, the eldest son of the team's fullback, Amy. She was a former Overtown street hooker who'd turned her life around by getting off drugs and buying a pizza franchise on fashionable Washington Avenue. Martin had already come up with a couple of hard-hitting stories about black-on-black gang violence in the Miami ghettoes and had secured a two-year contract to work as a trainee crime writer, reporting direct to the great Larry Coen.

Later, as Deborah drove back home in her convertible, crossing the MacArthur Causeway, she felt exhilarated as the endorphins flooded her body. In the inky sky, billions of stars decorated a humid November night.

* * *

The following morning Deborah was awoken by her cellphone.

'Sorry to interrupt your vacation.' It was Rico from investigations.

Deborah stretched. 'No problem. I was going to call Leroy later anyway to see what's going on.'

'We've had a woman pestering us since after eight, wanting to speak to you.'

'What about?'

'Wouldn't say. She just left her name and number, and asked me to get you to call her. She said she was the sister of Richard Turner. That mean anything to you?'

'Not off the top of my head,' Deborah lied. Rico gave her the number and she scribbled it down on a piece of scrap paper. 'Thanks, Rico. I'll be in touch.'

'Take it easy.'

Deborah did not hang around. Michelle Turner answered on the fourth ring.

'Deborah Jones.'

'Thanks for calling back. I really appreciate it. You discovered my brother's body?'

'Yes.'

'We need to talk. This thing has got way out of control. You need to know what exactly John found out.'

'I'm listening.'

'He sent something to Richard in an encrypted e-mail. But all his computers have been confiscated.'

'By who?'

'I don't know. I asked the police, but they said it was

95

nothing to do with them. Deborah, have you heard about the missing twenty-eight pages in the September 11 Congressional Report?'

'Sure.'

'Before he died Richard printed out some of the files that John had sent him, as a back-up. He said it was an insurance policy, in case the worst happened.'

'You're saying a hard copy was made? Do you have it?'

'Deborah, listen very carefully. I arrived in Miami this morning. I had planned to speak to you in person. But I got spooked. I was driving with the friend I'm staying with, and I sensed that someone was following us. I panicked, we headed off the freeway, and I decided to get rid of the documents.'

'You mean you've thrown them away?'

'Of course not. Does Opa-Locka mean anything to you? I paid six months in advance. Locker number sixty-two. The passcode to open it is one-five-four-three. You got that?'

Deborah scribbled down the number. 'Are you absolutely sure you were being followed?'

'Positive. A white guy. We lost him, I think. I hope.' Michelle's voice began to quiver. 'All I ask is that you let America know what's going on. I'm sorry, but—'

Suddenly the line went dead.

20

Deborah sat on her balcony, drinking iced tea and staring at what she'd scrawled on her notepad. *Locker 62. Passcode 1543.* She updated Sam on Michelle Turner but was disappointed by his frosty response.

Deborah would only get the go-ahead if Byron, the *Miami Herald*'s legal counsel, considered it okay for her to open the locker without the written permission of Michelle Turner.

'That's bullshit, Sam,' Deborah said, 'and you know it.'

'Maybe it is. But until I hear different, the investigation is on hold.'

From her balcony, Deborah stared out at the turquoise waters of the Atlantic. Breakers crashed onto the pristine beach. Life was going on as normal. Families kicking a ball, joggers, sun worshippers, dog walkers, lifeguards, children playing near their mothers. It seemed an age since she'd enjoyed walking along Ocean Drive, doing nothing for days on end except reading a good book, sitting in the shade of a palm tree in Lummus Park, jogging on the boardwalk, doing laps at the swimming pool in Flamingo Park, but most of all spending each and every day with Sam.

She went back inside, shut the French doors and walked into her bedroom, the air conditioning purring quietly in the background. She sat down at her desk and switched on her laptop.

For the rest of the day, using the Nexus system, she called up the latest articles from major papers across America, focusing primarily on the *New York Times* and *New York Daily News*. She was intrigued to spot the byline of an old Berkeley college buddy, Pam Molloy, who was now a crime reporter on the *News*. They had been close friends in San Francisco, both of them studying journalism, but had lost touch over the years.

Pam had done a story on Turner. She seemed to consider that this was the straightforward suicide of an old 1960s dope head. Curious to know if her old friend had any other leads, Deborah decided to give her a call.

'Hey, Miss Molloy,' Deborah said, 'congratulations on making it to the Big Apple.'

'Deborah, is that you?'

'Who do you think it is? Beyoncé?'

Pam laughed. 'And you're working at the mighty *Miami Herald*, is that right?'

'I'm investigations editor.'

'Get you. And you've got all that weather. Well, I have a one-bedroom shithole in Dumbo, Brooklyn. I'm freezing my butt off up here. But I guess, after all this time, you haven't called about the meteorological situation in New York.'

'That guy who died in the Brooklyn warehouse . . . ?' Deborah picked her way carefully. The NYPD hadn't revealed to the press that it was she who had discovered the body.

'Richard Turner.'

'That's the one.'

'You mind telling me why the *Miami Herald*'s investigations editor would be interested in him?'

'I'll owe you big time.'

'Okay, I won't press you. From what we can gather, he suffered mental health problems for years.'

'And police are satisfied about the cause of death?'

Deborah heard the rustling of papers.

'The autopsy was carried out by a Doctor Brent Simmons yesterday morning.' Alarm bells began ringing in Deborah's head.

'Look, thanks a million, Pam. That's fantastic – I've got to go now. I'll be in touch. And if you're ever in Miami, please let me know.'

'You can count on it.'

Dr Brent Simmons was the name of the Chief Medical Examiner in Miami-Dade, the same man who'd performed the autopsy on John Hudson.

Deborah keyed in the details of the Office of the Chief Medical Examiner in New York and hit 'Search'. It showed that the office was located at 520 First Avenue in Manhattan.

She dialed the number but didn't want to identify herself. 'Hi, sorry to bother you,' she said. 'Carla Romez at the *Miami Herald*. Just wanting to check our facts are correct. Can you tell me where Doctor Brent Simmons is located?'

'I'm sorry, Carla, you'll have to contact the city press office.'

Deborah groaned inwardly. 'We're just doing some fact-checking . . .'

'I'm sorry. You'll have to speak to Tom Russo in the press office. He deals with anything to do with the OCME.'

Deborah hung up and found the number of the mayor's press office off the New York City website.

Russo himself answered, his New York accent unmistakable.

'Tom, this is Carla Romez of the *Miami Herald*. How are you this afternoon?'

'Kinda hectic, Carla – you know how it gets.'

'Can you tell me, is there a Doctor Brent Simmons working within the Office of the Chief Medical Examiner, or employed as a pathologist by the city?'

'Simmons, huh? Let me see . . .'

Deborah was put on hold to the soft strains of Vivaldi's *Four Seasons*. She waited patiently for a couple of minutes.

'Did you say Simmons?' Eventually Russo came back on the line.

'Doctor Brent Simmons.'

'We got a Doctor Raul Simon working for us out of Queens. But definitely no Simmons.'

'I must have picked up the name wrong.'

'Maybe he worked for us in the past, but definitely not now.'

'This is a very recent case. Richard Turner, found dead in Brooklyn a few days ago. I was informed that Doctor Simmons conducted the autopsy. Just wanted to make sure that we've got our facts correct.'

'Hold on, Carla, I'll pull up the autopsy report – if it's in the system.'

Deborah was put back on Vivaldi.

'That's weird,' Russo said. 'Autopsy report 3749933–1. Carried out by Doctor Brent Simmons.'

Deborah scribbled down the autopsy report number beside Simmons's name. 'Is it possible that your Human Resources department might just be a little slow updating their files?'

'I guess it's possible, Carla. Tell you what I'll do, I'll contact the Chief Medical Examiner himself and see if he can shed any light on this.'

'I'd appreciate that, Tom.'

'Gimme your cellphone number and I'll call you back in a few minutes. How does that sound?'

'Perfect.'

Russo was as good as his word. 'I'm running into a

few problems here,' he said. 'The fact is I'm not too sure who conducted this autopsy.'

'Tom, I have it written down in black and white, as given to me by yourself a few minutes ago. Autopsy report three-seven-four-nine-nine-three-three-one for Richard Turner. Carried out by Doctor Brent Simmons. Even though you don't have anyone by that name employed by the Chief Medical Examiner's office. Am I missing something here, Tom?'

'Look, I'm really sorry. I can't say any more. I'd like to help. But I'm absolutely snowed under. Thanks so much for calling.'

Tom Russo did not wait for Deborah to say another word before he hung up on her.

21

The South Florida Evaluation and Treatment Center was a maximum-security forensic hospital located in a run-down area northwest of downtown Miami. It was only a twenty-five-minute drive from Nathan Stone's shabby room in Surfside, just off the Airport Expressway. But it was a journey he sometimes made two or three times a week when he was in town.

Nathan arrived at the main gate around mid-morning. He showed some ID and was patted down. Then he was allowed inside. Surveillance cameras were everywhere.

Fifteen minutes later he was sitting in a visitor room, holding hands with his sister who was crying as she usually did when they met. Helen's mascara was smudged. She wore a loose-fitting gray T-shirt, cargo shorts and new Nike sneakers he'd bought her. She always tried to make an effort for him. 'I'm sorry I missed my last visit, Helen, but you know how it is,' Nathan said, bending down to kiss her.

Helen smiled, her ghostly eyes tired and glazed. It had been that way for nearly thirty of her forty years. 'You always come back to see me, Nathan. Promise you won't ever leave me. Promise.'

Nathan kissed the back of her hand. 'You know I would never leave you, sis.' He leaned closer, lowering his voice. 'You'll never be alone, Helen, not as long as I live.' He brushed her auburn hair out of her eyes. She smelled of cigarettes and coffee. 'How are they treating you, Helen? You getting enough exercise? You eating well?'

'They're kind. I don't deserve such kindness. They let me watch whatever channel I want. And I can decide what *flavor* of ice cream I like. Not like in New York. They were so mean up there.'

Nathan felt his eyes brim with tears. He coughed, and brushed them away. He'd called in a few favors to get Helen transferred down to Miami about fifteen years ago, once it became clear that he was going to be based here.

'And I even have my own room. How great is that?'

'That's terrific,' he said. 'Nurses seem friendly too.'

'Did you know we're moving soon? I've asked for a room with a nice view. I want to see trees, animals, birds. That would be so cool, wouldn't it?'

Nathan nodded. He had already checked out the new site. The South Florida Evaluation and Treatment

Center was moving to a state-of-the-art facility at Homestead, thirty-five miles to the southwest of Miami, right on the edge of the Everglades. He made a mental note to speak to someone and get her the best room in the hospital. It was the least he could do.

Helen looked at him and smiled. 'You seeing a girl? Is that why you couldn't come?'

'I had a meeting. Schedules got mixed up. I'm real sorry.'

'I think they're working you too hard, Nathan. That's what I truly believe.'

'A man's got to work. Bills have to be paid.'

Helen stroked his hair, and then touched his cheek softly. It felt good. 'Got any cigarettes?'

'Gave them to Nurse Stevenson . . . outside.'

'Thank you, Nathan. I don't know what I'd do without you.' Helen stroked his cheek again. 'Someone's scratched you. Have you been fighting again?'

Nathan pulled away. 'It's nothing. A guy was being disrespectful to a lady in a bar, and I intervened.'

'Why are people so mean?'

Nathan shrugged and said nothing.

'Well, I'm glad that there are still good people around to stand up to bullies.'

For the next hour, Nathan sat and listened to her prattle on about the minutiae of her daily existence. The anti-psychotic drugs she was on, the clinical supervisor who was a great salsa dancer and seemed to have a crush on her, even the art classes she attended as part of her therapy program.

Nathan smiled and nodded. His heart was breaking.

Helen was the same little girl he'd looked after all those years ago in that rat-infested dump on the Lower East Side, cooking beans on a camping stove in the empty living room, tucking her up at night, while their father Al stayed away, drinking, and then sleeping all day. The only time they saw him was when the money he'd stolen had run out. One morning he came home in a blind fury and started hitting Nathan with his belt.

Nathan remembered tasting his own warm blood, and then seeing his sister – she was ten at the time – plunging a pair of scissors into his father's back. He watched Al collapse before Helen proceeded to stab him in the eyes and face, drenching herself in their father's blood until he stopped moving.

That morning was imprinted forever on Nathan's brain, and on Helen's. The doctors who examined her said that she was paranoid schizophrenic. She talked of hearing the voices of angels who had told her to do it.

Nathan started wetting the bed from the moment they were parted. He wanted to be with Helen. But they wouldn't allow it.

The days and weeks and months that followed were a succession of foster parents in and around the Tri-State Area, all unable or unwilling to deal with Nathan's violent mood swings.

The sound of his sister singing 'Somewhere Over the

Rainbow' snapped Nathan out of his reverie. He took hold of her hands. 'I'll never leave you.'

'Promise.'

'I promise.'

As Nathan walked out of the hospital he was relieved to feel the warm sun on his skin and see blue skies above. His sister would forever remain trapped in the past. And so would he.

22

The Joseph H. Davis Center for Forensic Pathology was located in downtown Miami. The Chief Medical Examiner's department was right across the street from the Jackson Memorial Hospital's Ryder Trauma Center.

Deborah crossed the stifling street and walked through lushly landscaped gardens to the building.

Inside, huge windows allowed natural light to flow in and the air conditioning was a welcome relief. Oak trims were everywhere and smart carpets and artwork adorned the lobby. The centerpiece was a three-storey staircase that led to an atrium, with a huge skylight above.

Deborah introduced herself to a freckled receptionist.

'Just take a seat. Dr Simmons will be with you in a minute.'

Deborah chose a brown leather sofa and wondered how long she'd have to wait. Twenty-nine minutes ticked slowly by. She flicked through that day's *Herald*. So much about Iraq. Stories about corruption among contractors, the death of a Fort Lauderdale soldier, another 'surge' to take the fight to the insurgents and more horrendous suicide bombings.

'Miss Jones.'

Deborah looked up. Standing before her, wearing an immaculate gray suit, white shirt and maroon tie, was Dr Simmons, a name tag round his neck. She stood up and shook his hand. 'Good of you to see me at such short notice, sir.'

'No problem.' His smile reminded her of her father's.

They took the elevator to the second floor, engaging in small talk about the sub-prime mortgage crisis that was sweeping the country.

The floor-to-ceiling windows in Dr Simmons's office had a panoramic view of the Miami skyline, glistening in the morning sun. Simmons sat down behind his desk while Deborah took out her tape recorder, notepad and pens. 'You don't mind if I keep a record of this conversation, I hope?' she asked.

'No problem, Miss Jones.'

'My shorthand isn't what it used to be.'

Dr Simmons smiled. 'Well, we doctors have the worst handwriting among all professions, as you know.'

'Okay, we're ready to go, Doctor Simmons. First of all, thanks again for seeing me at such short notice. But we're looking for some clarification.'

Dr Simmons raised an eyebrow.

'Into the autopsy of John Hudson.'

Dr Simmons nodded.

'I believe it was carried out here, is that right?'

'Do you mind me asking what is the precise purpose of your questions? I believe you are the investigations editor of the *Miami Herald*?'

'That's correct. We're looking into the deaths of John Hudson and a friend of his called Richard Turner.'

The doctor's face remained impassive.

'Can you tell me about the autopsy that was carried out on John Hudson?'

'We're still running some tests, so I can't say anything definite at this stage. And obviously, we have to be mindful of the family.'

'Of course. I believe my boss, Sam Goldberg, an old friend of Bill Hudson, met you shortly after the body was brought in.'

'That's right.'

'My second question is this: we've been told by someone within the media office for the Chief Medical Examiner in New York City that the autopsy of Richard Turner was also carried out by Doctor Brent Simmons. Subsequently this assertion was retracted. I wondered if you would care to comment?'

'How very bizarre. It must've been a mix-up of names.'

'The press office had no record of you.'

'That's the craziest thing I've heard. It's out of my jurisdiction. I've not been to New York for months. I think the last time I was there was for a conference way back in March. My secretary could confirm the dates if you'd like.'

'So you never carried out the autopsy in New York?'

'Absolutely not.' Dr Simmons smiled, as if waiting for another question.

'I've got the autopsy report number on Richard Turner. That report would have the name of the medical examiner on it.'

'Of course. But, frankly, nothing surprises me these days what with the amount of administration, form-filling and God knows what new regulations that we're all supposed to follow. It's never-ending. The miracle is that we get any real work done at all.'

23

Simmons's casual explanation rankled with Deborah. She didn't buy it. She trawled through public records and, with some help from McNally's contacts, compiled a 115-page dossier on Dr Brent Simmons, the Chief Medical Examiner in Miami-Dade. It contained everything from his birth certificate, school reports and college grades right up until his current employment.

Deborah fixed herself a turkey sandwich on rye and a glass of mineral water. She felt better after the food, and then she got down to business.

The autopsy report on Richard Turner revealed that it had apparently been undertaken by Dr Ken T. Meiter, the medical examiner assigned to Brooklyn.

She called Sam immediately with the news.

'Sometimes, Deborah,' Sam said, 'things aren't exactly as they seem.'

'You sound like Fox Mulder.'

'Does the name Roger Mittleman ring any bells?'

'Of course. He was the Miami-Dade medical examiner a few years back.' She suddenly made the connection. 'He once altered an autopsy report, didn't he?'

'He removed the fact that traces of marijuana were found in the body of Mayor Miscon's wife.'

'Are you saying that this autopsy report has been doctored?'

'I don't know. It's possible.'

'There's something not right here. I know it.'

'Perhaps. Look, I've got stuff to do. Let's speak later. I love you.'

'Love you too, Sam.'

Deborah worked her way through the rest of the file.

Brent Simmons had been educated at the private St Leonard's Episcopal School, Albany, New York, leaving in 1967 with a high school diploma. He then went to Levington College, in Boston, and achieved an Associates Degree in Liberal Arts, in 1971. Three years later, he'd graduated with a Bachelor of Science, from the University of Texas, Austin. Five years later – 1979 – he was a medical doctor after studying at the University of Vermont Medical School, Burlington.

Next, he did an internship at All Saint's Hospital in Tampa, Florida – six months in internal medicine, six months general surgery. Afterwards, he took up residency in the Department of Anatomic and Clinical Pathology at Brown University, Rhode Island.

Deborah was impressed. This man was highly qualified, and highly intelligent.

She read on.

Simmons's educational path then moved to Miami where he specialized in forensic pathology with his current employer, the Miami-Dade County Medical Examiner Department.

In 1985 Dr Brent Simmons became Associate Medical Examiner, teaching at the University of Miami School of Medicine. His position was Assistant Clinical Professor of Pathology. He also lectured abroad extensively.

Deborah scanned through pages outlining his membership of elite professional groups – American Academy of Forensic Sciences, National Association of Medical Examiners. And then there were the awards. Teaching awards, certificates of appreciation, exceptional-service award from the Miami-Dade Police, and on and on.

Two hours later, Deborah was barely a third of the way through the dossier. She knew she'd have to call Faith, her soccer coach, who wanted the team in for extra training that evening, ahead of a big game.

She punched in the cellphone number. Faith answered in her usual cheery voice. 'Hey, honey, what's happening with my favorite striker?'

'I don't think I'm going to be your favorite anything for much longer. Faith, I'm sorry, I have to cancel tonight.'

'Why, for Christ's sake?'

'I'm working on something. And I just can't put it to one side.'

'You ain't never missed no practice session before. Why start now? Next time I see you, you better have on your T-shirt and shorts or you ain't never gonna play for us again. Is that understood?'

'I promise.'

'Hey, you ain't two-timing me for that fine young Mr Goldberg?'

Deborah laughed. 'If only,' she said.

24

The smell of stale coffee lingered in the conference room. Sam Goldberg sat alone, following the afternoon news meeting. He felt quite drained after ninety minutes of heated arguments.

Sam had always relished the cut and thrust of negotiating what went in the paper and what was left out. Today he had sat quietly as Metro put their case that a five-year-old Hispanic boy who'd been dubbed the 'Mozart of Miami' by a famous Russian conductor deserved a front-page slot, while the Foreign Desk pressed hard for an urgent reappraisal of the situation in Afghanistan.

When Larry Coen mentioned the John Hudson police investigation Sam didn't bat an eyelid. Had his judgment been clouded because of his personal relationship with a member of staff, and indeed, because he was also the victim's godfather? Would he have allowed any other senior journalist to ignore Juan or Harry's instructions?

Sam stood up and looked down over the city. The dark blue waters of Biscayne were choppy after a near-miss hurricane. He spotted a couple of dolphins swimming against the tide, not a care in the world. He really fancied a drink.

There was a knock at the door.

Hablo Ferrer came in, holding a cup of coffee. 'You got a few minutes, Sam?' he asked.

Sam shrugged. 'Sure.'

Hablo pulled up a seat next to Sam and placed his coffee on the table. He adjusted his red braces. 'I just want to clear the air. You need to know my side of the story.'

Sam shrugged.

'We've been working for a long time on a story about Cuban spies coming ashore in speedboats with their families, claiming they're fleeing Castro. My source is someone I've known for fifteen years. He asks me where he can reach Juan. When I ask why, he tells me about Deborah and this Turner guy. He's concerned that she might have compromised something they had been working on for months. I gave him Juan's cellphone number, and that was that.'

Sam said nothing.

'I was not trying to undermine you, I swear,' Hablo said. He took a sip of his coffee. 'Believe me on that.'

Sam sighed. 'Couldn't you have spoken to me first?'

'Perhaps. But I don't answer to you, Sam.'

'You're still smarting that it was the *Miami Herald* that exposed those payments . . .'

'Sam, as you know, the three journalists who were fired were taken back.'

'After an outcry in the Cuban-American community in Miami.'

'Know what pisses you off, Sam? Miami is no longer the city you knew when you grew up. Is that what this is all about? It's changing all the time, whilst you're stuck in the past. This is a Latino city, and my paper reflects that.'

Sam's cellphone rang, interrupting the exchange. 'Let's just agree to disagree, okay?' He looked at the caller display and saw that it was his sister. 'Look, I need to have some privacy for this call, if you don't mind.'

As he left the conference room, Hablo muttered under his breath, 'You really are an asshole'.

'How are you, Lauren?' It was the first time in a week Sam had spoken to his sister.

'Don't think I'll be touching oysters again.'

'Look, I'm sorry I've not been up for a couple of weeks, but—'

'Sam, you don't have to explain. You've got your hands full, I know. I read about Bill Hudson's boy. Terrible!'

'I'd rather not talk about it.'

'Sure. Listen, only a quick call. Miriam just called to say that it'll soon be Joel's bar mitzvah. And she's wanting the whole family up there.'

'When?'

'In a couple of weeks. It's a Friday night.'

'In Scattle?'

'Where else?'

'Shit . . . I've got a million and one things to attend to.'

Lauren sighed. 'Sam, Miriam's counting on you. She's your sister. You have to go. It's the rules.'

'Who says? It's not even her son, for chrissakes. It's her stepson.'

'Oh come on, Sam, don't be so mean.'

'Lauren, we haven't talked for nearly two years. Maybe more.'

'It was one of your dumb throwaway remarks, wasn't it?'

Sam smiled. 'I think I may have mentioned, just in passing, a joke about Bill Clinton and his penchant for Jewish interns.'

Lauren laughed. 'You know how she is, Sam. She's very thin-skinned. But she's got a good heart. Besides, she's very happy just now.'

'Unlike her husband. Every time we meet up, he can barely string a sentence together. He's one sullen asshole.'

'Maybe. Look, Sam, Miriam'll be devastated if you and Deborah can't make it. You need to do this.'

'This is crazy. I've not even had an invite. And why isn't she calling me?'

'She wanted to. But she's scared that you'll turn her down flat. She asked me to talk to you.'

Sam sighed. 'I don't know . . . look, I'll think about it, okay?'

'I'm asking you really nicely, Sam, to forget about any

argument you've had with her in the past, and enjoy a great bar mitzvah. Joel's a lovely boy. You'll like him. He wants to be an editor, just like you.'

Sam said nothing.

'Miriam's always looked up to you, Sam. Even more than I do. Just say yes.'

'You're a pain in the ass, do you know that?'

'So, can I tell her you'll both be there?'

Sam let out a long sigh, thinking of his horrendous workload. He couldn't afford to take any time off in the next month. But then he thought of Miriam's ghostly, anxious face, trying to explain to her cold fish of a husband why Sam couldn't manage to get away for his beloved Joel's bar mitzvah. 'Lauren, tell Miriam from me that I wouldn't miss it for the world.'

25

Just after nine p.m. Harry Donovan had settled down on the living-room sofa with a glass of Merlot to watch Larry King interviewing Barbara Walters on CNN – his wife fast asleep after popping her nightly Ambien sleeping pills – when his cellphone rang.

'Harry Donovan,' he groaned, hoping the interruption wouldn't wake Jacqueline.

'Can we talk?' It was Rebecca.

'Are you out of your goddamn mind?' Harry hissed. 'What have I always said?'

'I had to call you. I'm scared. There's a prowler outside.'

'What?'

'I'm looking out of my apartment, towards the gate-house, and he's smoking a goddamn cigarette. He's wearing a baseball cap.'

'Where's the guard?'

'Off sick.'

'Call 911. Now!'

'Harry, the police already came round fifteen minutes ago. But this is the second time I've seen him. Harry, please. Can you come over? The cops'll think I'm nuts if I call again.'

'Gimme five minutes. And lock your doors and windows. I'm on my way.'

Harry picked up his car keys and sped the two miles to the smart enclave on the northern tip of Key Biscayne. He slowed down beside the empty gatehouse – its barrier was raised – wondering if the man was still around. He parked next to Rebecca's metallic silver Honda, the car he'd bought her.

He got out of his own car and walked across the parking lot, looking around. The air was humid and warm, and his shirt was already sticking to his back. He bent down to look under the parked cars and then peered into the darkness to check for any movement in or around the rear of the building. Nothing.

Satisfied that there was no one around now, he buzzed Rebecca's apartment and was let in.

Rebecca was shaking and he put his arms around her. 'It's okay, I'm here. You're gonna be fine.'

Rebecca held him tight for a couple of seconds too long before she extricated herself from his embrace. Then she went across to the lounge windows overlooking the parking lot and pointed at the gatehouse. 'I swear he was staring up at me, both times,' she said.

'Are you sure?'

'What, you think I made this up?'

Harry shook his head.

'The cops came and didn't see anything.'

'Could you make out his face?'

'He was white, I think. Dolphins baseball cap, but it was dark and the palms around the gatehouse obscured his features.'

Harry pulled out his cellphone from his pocket and dialed 911. 'Hi, this is the residence of Rebecca Sinez at Ocean Park Drive. The prowler returned after your guys left, but he seems to have disappeared once again into thin air. I need you to send round a car and do one more sweep.'

The dispatcher, a woman, was helpful. 'Sir, they're on their way. Sit tight. Are you a friend of Ms Sinez?'

'You could say that.'

'I'd appreciate if you could stay right there. Is that okay?'

'No problem at all.'

The police arrived in under a minute. Harry and Rebecca peered down to the parking lot as the cops searched the area with flashlights. But they didn't find anything, not even a cigarette butt.

The officers said they'd keep a car nearby all night, which pacified Rebecca and Harry. When they left, Rebecca buried her head in her hands.

'What's going on, Harry?'

'I wish to God I knew.'

'You think this is connected to . . .'

'What?'

'The investigation. Is that what this is?'

'I don't know.'

'It's like a nightmare.'

'Hang on, this might all be perfectly innocent, so let's not get too carried away.'

'It might seem perfectly innocent to you, but coming so soon after the guy taking pictures of my son . . . *our* goddamn son at the beach, what am I supposed to think?'

'Keep your voice down. Look, you were the one who was against me going to the feds about this. Have you changed your mind now?'

Rebecca dropped her gaze to the floor.

'Just say the word and I'll let the authorities know. Is that what you want?'

'I don't know.'

'I'll stay here tonight if you want.'

'It's okay.'

'How about if I sit outside in the car. Would that make you feel better?'

'Would you do that?'

Harry held her hand and smiled. 'I only want what's best for you and Andrew, that's all.'

He waited until just after 10.30 p.m. and after kissing his son as he slept he left quietly, doing another quick sweep of the parking lot. But again he found nothing. He got into his car, watching for anything untoward in the shadows. The only sound was his own breathing.

He glanced up and saw the blinds being drawn in Rebecca's lounge, thinking of his flesh and blood sound asleep under his Spider-Man duvet. But instead of heading home he just sat and watched and waited.

Harry switched on a Miami talk-radio channel and listened as the host and the callers talked about everything from the budget deficit to gay marriages.

It was going to be a long night.

26

It was late and Deborah was reading the dossier on Simmons. Letterman was on the TV with the sound down when Sam called.

'Fancy a bite to eat?'

'Sam, do you know what time it is?'

'I can't sleep. Besides, I'd like to relax for an hour or two. What do you say?'

'I'd love to see you, Sam. You know that, but I've got work to do.'

'Join the club.'

It was really buzzing on the terrace of Emeril's. Deborah laughed a lot and Sam quickly gave up grimacing every time he took a sip of his Badois sparkling water. The night was luxuriantly warm.

When they kissed, a couple nearby shook their heads.

That made them laugh some more, like a young couple on their first serious date.

Deborah looked into Sam's eyes. He smiled and reached out for her hand. On Collins, only yards away, was the typical hustle and bustle of South Beach – SUVs pumping out bass-heavy rap, tourists soaking up the vibes and the full moon shimmering on the inky waters of the Atlantic in the distance. Gulls were swooping low for scraps on the beach.

'I had a dream last night,' she said.

'A good one, I hope.'

'I was down on the beach, and I was trying to catch up with you and was trying to call you. But you were out of earshot. I kept on shouting but every time I got closer you just kept walking. Just out of reach.'

Sam smiled. 'I have a very practical suggestion,' he said.

Deborah sat still on the sofa, listening to Sam's heavy breathing as he slept. She stroked his graying hair. A hint of his aftershave lingered in the air. She sighed, letting the late-night music wash over her. It was Bill Evans, the melancholy jazz pianist, recorded live at the legendary Village Vanguard. She had felt ready but Sam seemed quite content to just lie with her, holding her tight. Which was fine, in itself. But she longed for him to make the first move. Was she giving out the wrong signals? Perhaps she should have taken the lead, although she still felt horribly self-conscious about the scars on her back.

It was just after one, and Deborah was not in the least bit tired. It was very out of character for Sam to have suggested coming over to her place. But he hadn't taken the final step. Maybe he was afraid of something too?

In the early days of the relationship he had tried to be more physical, but she had rejected his advances. Now she bitterly regretted it. But it had taken a long time to trust him, to feel convinced that he really did love her.

It was nearly seven years since his wife had died of cancer. Sam rarely talked about her. He had stacked all the pictures of her in the attic. Occasionally, Deborah wondered how she compared. He must have thought about it too.

She watched him for a while and experienced a great wave of tenderness. His tie was undone and there were shadows under his eyes. She was glad his hard-drinking days had stopped but she knew how tough it must be for him.

At the *Herald* he worked himself and his team very hard. Newspapers had been his life for almost a quarter of a century, since he had graduated from the University of Miami. He'd helped transform Deborah from a shy, retiring feature writer, specializing in fluffy pieces about celebrities jetting in and out of the South Beach hot spots, into a highly respected investigative journalist.

He'd backed her initial interest in William Craig, the elderly Scot on Florida's death row, but nobody, least of all Deborah, could have foreseen where that case would lead. When Craig was released, it made her name and cemented her reputation as she unearthed exclusives revealing that Joe O'Neill – the son of ex-Senator Jack O'Neill – had been a serial rapist before Craig had killed him.

Sam stirred and it looked for a moment as if he might wake up. He had taken off his shoes earlier and now lay stretched out on the sofa. Deborah fetched a blanket and draped it over him. Then she kissed him gently on the forehead.

27

Just after three a.m., unable to sleep, Deborah shut the lounge door and went into her bedroom and through to her spacious en-suite bathroom. She turned on the taps and tipped in a liberal dose of bath salts. Then she lit a few jasmine- and lime-scented candles and switched off the lights to achieve the Zenlike calm that she craved. She switched on the nearby radio and some sweeping orchestral work filled the bathroom.

As Deborah immersed herself in the warm water she groaned and closed her eyes. The smell of eucalyptus salts mingled with the jasmine and lime that infused the steamy air. She felt her neck and shoulder muscles starting to relax.

The music was spiriting her away to another world.

She found herself thinking of idyllic childhood picnics at Bienville, splashing in the tannin waters, sitting on the homemade blanket. Then chicken club sandwiches, slices of apple pie, soda and laughter. Her mother handed out the food as Deborah and her brother squabbled over who was eating what. And all the while her father smiled at them, occasionally quoting from the Bible that he carried at all times.

She thought of a sun-kissed beach where she and Sam would stroll, lie in the sun and make love. She was ready. At last. She imagined calypso music and the sound of children laughing in the distance. The gentle roar as the surf ran up the shallow-shelving beach. Out on the ocean a few gaily-painted small fishing boats bobbed around, waiting to bring in their nets.

Deborah suddenly opened her eyes and gasped. Standing above her, wearing a black mask across the top of his face, was a man. He was smiling, his lips curling grimly, as the music reached a crescendo.

Reaching down, he grabbed her by the throat, lifting her clean out of the bath and slamming her against the tiled wall. She struggled to breathe. The man's dark eyes glared at her through the eyeholes of the mask. She had rehearsed what she would do if ever a man attacked her but now she was frozen by fear, her legs shaking, tears spilling down her face.

'One sound and you die,' he said.

Deborah thought she was going to pass out.

'Take this as a warning. Forget about Hudson, or someone is gonna suffer like they've never suffered before. Is that clear?'

'Yes,' Deborah croaked.

The man loosened his grip and she fell to the floor on her knees, clutching her neck.

'You will tell no one about what I've said. No one. And you must not go to the police. If you do, your brother and his pretty young wife are going to regret they were born. You remember what those two boys did to you back in San Francisco? Imagine what I will do to your sister-in-law. And trust me, I have a thing for colored women.'

The man looked down at Deborah, his pupils like black pinpricks as she cowered on the floor, terror flooding her veins. Suddenly, out of the corner of her eye, she saw Sam.

Please help me.

Sam launched himself at the masked intruder, slamming him down onto the hardwood floor. For a few seconds they grappled and traded punches, trying to get the upper hand as Deborah watched, paralyzed with fear. But, quick as a flash, the man grabbed Sam's throat with a huge hand. Then he pressed his fingers tight into Sam's windpipe, attempting to choke him. Sam's face went purple.

Deborah felt an incredible surge of adrenalin. And she flew at the masked man, clawing at his eyes. He swore as she drew blood. Then he released Sam who collapsed in a heap. Half blinded, the masked, bloodied intruder lashed out, catching Deborah on the side of the face.

She was knocked backwards into the bath, her head

under the water. For a few moments, disorientated and petrified, she realized she was partially submerged in the warm soapy water. Then she surfaced, gasping for air.

The man stood looking down at her, grinning.

Deborah grabbed a candle and thrust it upwards into the side of his mask. She could smell the wool burn and then his skin. Clutching at his face, he staggered and fell to the floor

Wet and naked, Deborah jumped out of the bath and tried to pull a semi-conscious Sam to safety, blood rushing to her head in blind panic. He was like a dead weight. But anger and fear came to her aid. She was moving him, inch by slippery inch, into the bedroom.

A sharp kick from the intruder caught the back of her calf and her legs gave way. Deborah yelped at the pain and twisted awkwardly on the floor.

The man was back on his feet, his teeth clenched. His bloodied eyes, glistening with rage, were inches from her face, and his nostrils were dripping with blood. He reached down and tightened his grip on her throat. She felt the life draining from her.

Noticing in her peripheral vision that Sam was trying to move, Deborah summoned up all her reserves of strength and kneed the masked man hard in the groin. He grunted and momentarily released his grip.

Frantic, Deborah spotted on the floor a cosmetics bag which had been knocked over in the struggle. A metal nail file stuck out of the side. She grabbed hold of it, reached up and plunged it deep into the man's thigh.

'Bastard!' she cried.

Blood spurted onto the hardwood floor.

Undeterred, the man yanked out the nail file and tossed it aside. Deborah tried to scramble away but he was too quick. He kicked her in the ribs. She went sprawling against the bedroom wall.

Then he kicked her square on the jaw. She lay motionless in acute pain, still conscious.

With one hand the masked man picked up Sam by the neck and smashed him face down onto the floor.

The man turned and smiled before bending to yank Deborah up by the hair. 'You've had it easy this time,' he said. 'No further warnings will be given.'

Then everything went black.

28

Nathan Stone was seething. He pulled off his blood-soaked mask as he stood over the naked body of Deborah Jones. There was more that he would have liked to do, but that wasn't his remit. Perhaps the next time . . .

Taking out his cellphone, he snapped several photos which he then e-mailed to his laptop at his motel and to his handler. He took a couple more of Sam Goldberg, whose blood was congealing around his nose.

Stone knelt down beside Deborah's body and rolled her over. He saw the scars on her back that she'd received from the men who had attacked her years earlier at Berkeley. He allowed himself the pleasure of feeling the grooves they'd carved into her skin.

Then he reached for his cellphone again.

29

It took Deborah several moments to gather her thoughts as she came to. She was lying naked and cold on the bare wooden floor. Her head was throbbing. She tried to sit up, and nearly fell back in shock as she saw the body sprawled in the bedroom.

Deborah crawled over to Sam and felt a faint pulse.

'Sam, wake up, please,' she said. 'Sam Goldberg, wake up! Right now! It's Deborah!'

Sam didn't move.

Deborah tried hard not to panic. 'Sam!' she shouted. 'Wake up – come on, now. This is Deborah. Do you hear me? I said, do you hear me?'

Nothing.

'Sam, open your eyes.' Her voice caught slightly, breaking with emotion. 'Please!'

He stirred slightly, his eyes flickering open for a moment. But then they closed again.

'Just relax, Sam,' she said, holding his hand, and stroking his bloodied hair. 'It's gonna be okay. Stay with me.'

But Sam said nothing. Deborah called 911 from her bedside phone.

A minute or so later armed cops were swarming all over the house. Then paramedics.

The short journey from South Beach in the back of an ambulance with a uniformed policewoman seemed to take a lifetime. Sam's head was encased in a hard plastic support and he was wearing an oxygen mask. Deborah gripped his hand as the siren wailed and the ambulance cut through light traffic on the MacArthur Causeway. But Sam's eyes remained tight shut.

30

After giving a lengthy statement to police Deborah spent an age waiting in the hospital corridor. Eventually an ashen-faced young trauma doctor called Orieto emerged from the emergency room where they were working on Sam. He escorted Deborah to his office and sat her down.

'There's not an easy way to tell you this,' he said. 'Mr Goldberg is not responding the way we would have liked.'

All Deborah could do was nod.

'Technically he is now classified as in a coma. The next twenty-four hours are going to be crucial. They always are. Perhaps we will see some kind of response, may be to a voice. But at the moment . . .'

'What are his chances, honestly, doctor?'

'The CT scans and MRI came back clear – no swelling on the brain, which is obviously good.'

'Is he going to survive or not?'

'He is fighting for his life as we speak.'

'You need to get him better. Do you hear me?'

'We are doing everything we can. You can come and see him now.'

Sam's eyes were shut and a respirator tube was taped to his mouth. The Trauma Intensive Care Unit nurse who was checking a monitor said, 'Just sit down, stroke his hand, talk to him.'

Deborah took his left hand. 'Hi, Sam, it's only me.'

She pressed the nail of her thumb into the palm of his hand. Nothing.

'Now listen hard, Sam, we are going to get you through this. I will not accept anything else, do you hear me?'

The nurse gave a weak smile and left the room.

'Sam, are you listening? You're alive, and you're in the best goddamn hospital in Florida. Don't leave me now. We've got the best years of our life ahead of us, and I'll be damned if I'm going to spend them alone.'

Throughout the night, Deborah sat holding Sam's hand, while the respirator hummed in the background. She stayed there until the pale orange sun shone through the blinds.

31

Harry Donovan had spent all night sitting awake in his car outside Rebecca's condo. By first light he was physically and mentally exhausted. Now he felt sick as Deborah told him about the attack.

Would he be next? he wondered.

After clicking off his cellphone he headed straight to the second floor of the Ryder Trauma Center, adjacent to the hospital's Emergency Care Center, where the twenty-bed intensive care unit was located.

He stayed for nearly an hour with Deborah at Sam's bedside. Afterwards, the hospital's antiseptic smell still in his nostrils, he headed into the office and locked his door.

For ten long minutes he sat in silent contemplation, trying to work out what the hell to do. The first thing he did was call an emergency meeting of the senior executives in the conference room, ahead of the morning news meeting. He put Metro editor Ricky Garcia in charge of putting out the following day's *Herald*. Then he left them to it and returned to the sanctuary of his office, telling his PA he didn't want to be disturbed.

Harry then called Juan.

'What're his chances?'

'Not good. Deborah's hanging in, though.'

'Put her on indefinite compassionate leave. She needs to be with Sam, not to worry about goddamn investigations. Look, keep me informed if there's any change in Sam's condition. I'm on my way back. I'll inform the board myself. And try and keep this quiet. The networks and all the press will go apeshit.'

Harry punched in the only number stored in his cellphone that he had never called before. Only in an emergency, he'd been told. Well, this was an emergency. He was disappointed to be diverted to voicemail.

Over the next hour he tried several more times but without success. He went back to the hospital just after lunch but there was no sign of improvement in Sam's condition. Deborah was being comforted by two rather burly female friends who played in the same soccer team.

Afterwards, Harry returned to the office where he fielded tearful calls from Sam's two sisters and had a brief meeting with Ricky who was clearly feeling the strain.

'You need to tell the rest of the staff, Harry,' he said. 'The rumor mill is in full flow.'

The newsroom was hushed as Harry spoke. Apart from the sound of his voice there was only the occasional fax machine whirring or phone ringing unanswered to be heard. His message was brief and to the point.

Whatever happened, Sam was a newspaperman first and foremost. The rest of them had to do their jobs. He would expect nothing less.

Back in his office, Harry tried the number again. This time there was an answer.

'Sorry to call,' he said. 'It's Harry Donovan of the *Miami Herald*. Look, I have a problem. We need to talk.'

There was a slight hesitation. 'I'm out of the country . . . can't this wait?'

'Someone knows about Andrew. How is that possible? You told me no one would ever—'

'Hold on, Harry. What are you talking about?'

'I want to keep my personal life private. I thought that was part of the deal.' Harry explained the situation.

'Okay, okay. I'll put in some calls. If it's someone at my end, then they are in deep shit. I'll get to the bottom of this. We value you, Harry.'

'I hope you do. Because if I don't get some answers and reassurances I will be going straight to the feds about this. Do you understand me? Deal or no deal.'

'Don't do anything rash, Harry. That would not be a good idea. I'll get back to you by the end of the day.'

Harry called back just before six. But this time the tone of the man at the other end wasn't conciliatory. 'This is far more complicated than I thought at first,' he said.

'So what's the bottom line?'

'Harry, I say this as a friend,' the man replied, clearing his throat, 'but there are powers at work here over which we have no control. I cannot protect you anymore. I'm sorry. You need to do what is right for your family.'

'So that's it, then? You're cutting me loose?'

'Don't call this number again. I can't help you. You're on your own.'

32

The dark sky outside the hospital window was beginning to lighten. Slowly, miraculously, Sam began to open his eyes, as if he was afraid of what he'd see.

Deborah gazed at him for several moments. Then she smiled and kissed the back of his hand.

'It's okay,' she said. 'You're back. And you're safe.'

Sam stared at her. Then gave a small nod.

Deborah leaned close and kissed his unshaven cheek. 'I knew you wouldn't leave me, Sam.'

There was a flicker of his distinctive world-weary smile.

Deborah immediately rang the bell beside the monitor. A few moments later there was a flurry of activity as the medical team checked his chart, the monitors and the ventilator and decided on a new set of assessments.

'What the hell happened?' she heard Sam croak.

* * *

The arrival of Sam's sisters Lauren and Miriam was a big relief for Deborah. They hugged her and thanked her for never leaving him before they sat either side of their brother, holding a hand each as he lay back and smiled at them. Deborah was close to exhaustion. But she remained with Sam's sisters, content to watch over him, stroking his hair and telling him everything was going to be all right.

But Deborah did make sure to call the *Herald*.

In no time at all, a buoyant Harry Donovan turned up, regaling Sam and his sisters with old newsroom gossip. Then he had to dash back for the usual morning meeting. 'The news doesn't wait for an old news-paperman playing hookey,' he said with a grin as he closed the door.

A short while later Byron, the *Herald*'s legal counsel, turned up. He didn't stay longer than the regulation fifteen minutes, and Deborah accompanied him to the elevators.

'Thank God he made it,' Byron said. 'The place is not the same without him. Or you, for that matter.' He squeezed her arm. 'Get some shut-eye. You look like you need it. Oh, and tell Sam,' he said, as the elevator doors opened, 'that he got the go-ahead.'

'Go-ahead for what?'

'Opa-Locka. We checked things over. It's all fine.'

Deborah's decision to get back to work was met with incredulity by Faith. Unable to persuade her to reconsider, she insisted that Jamille Powers, who'd visited the hospital the previous night, accompany her and stay with her too.

Although welcoming the idea, Deborah felt slightly intimidated by the six-foot Overtown goalkeeper, a former kick-boxing champion who had worked in the late 1990s as a bodyguard for Jennifer Lopez and Cher. Prior to that she had been a tough street hooker in her neighborhood. But she had cleaned up her act, like all the soccer girls, and now had a Master's in political science from the University of Miami and was in the final year of her PhD. According to Faith, Jamille's IQ was 'off the scale', although she always 'carried her little gun, just for emergencies.'

Meanwhile the apartment had been cleaned up by Faith and the girls, the locks changed. Deborah recharged her cellphone and after a quick shower she put on some fresh clothes – T-shirt, jeans and sneakers. Then she went down with Jamille to the car.

Opa-Locka had been built in the 1920s and boasted some of the finest Moorish architecture in the world. Minarets, domes and outdoor staircases dominated the city skyline, but the days of grand visions in this forgotten outpost of Miami were long gone. Now Opa-Locka was synonymous with despair, drugs and gang violence.

Dusty palms lined the streets and graffiti adorned shuttered shops, but the street dealers and gangs were nowhere to be seen so early in the day.

It had been a picture-postcard town when it had first been built, but all that had changed once the US Navy shut down its base at Opa-Locka airport. The slow decline had begun in the 1960s. The white middle classes had moved out, and the poor blacks had moved in.

Crack cocaine had transformed the area at night into a war zone, especially the Triangle, a nine-block hellhole torn apart by gangs toting AK-47s. Recently a young mother who'd gone out to get milk for her child had been shot dead by an anonymous sniper. Also, a five-year-old girl, whose family had been fleeing the area with a police escort, had been killed by a sniper's rifle – drug gangs fired at anything that moved.

The secure self-storage facility was situated just off Railroad Drive, five blocks from Duval, a notorious intersection with Lincoln Avenue. Drive-by killings there were commonplace. The place even attracted gangsters from Carol City, trying to make a name for themselves.

Jamille's car jolted over a pothole. 'Goddamn it,' she muttered.

She accelerated down 22nd Avenue past run-down housing complexes, then down 152nd Street near the railway line – windows barred, disintegrating sofas rotting on sun-bleached front yards – and then along Railroad Drive.

A billboard for the secure self-storage facility indicated that they were 'only 500 yards away'.

The vast parking lot was empty, except for one car. This was no state-of-the-art facility swept by security cameras and patrolled by guards.

A young black man wearing an ill-fitting suit was nodding his head behind the security glass. He took off his earphones when he noticed the two women.

'Here to pick up some of my things.'

'Got ID?'

Deborah shook her head.

'Sorry, ladies, but I can't let you in. Company rules. Very strict on that.'

'Look, it's for a friend. I've got the passcode.'

'Like I said, we got rules. And the rules say if you ain't the keyholder, you ain't getting in. End of discussion.'

'Gimme a break, will you? This is important.'

The young man just shrugged. 'Sorry, lady, but it ain't my problem.'

Jamille stepped forward and smiled. 'Tell me, honey, what's your name?'

'Reggie Purcell, ma'am.'

'You from around here?'

'No, ma'am. Hialeah. Born and bred.'

'Thought you looked familiar. You're cute. Didn't we hook up at that big party thrown in Hialeah couple of years back? If I remember right, you said you lived on East 56th Street.'

'You must've gotten me mixed up with someone else, ma'am.'

'No, I'm good with faces. I distinctly remember you

saying you lived two doors down and that there had been a double shooting three days earlier. Kinda freaked me out. I asked you to walk me home.'

The young man gave a shy grin and casually scratched the back of his head. 'I don't think so. I live with my folks on East 8th Street. Sorry to disappoint.'

'So you're not going to help us, is that what you're saying?'

'You got it.'

'Okay, we'll see about that.' Jamille turned away and pulled out her cellphone. Then she punched in a few numbers.

'I'm sorry – what are you doing?' Reggie said behind the glass.

'Calling your head office to complain about your attitude.'

'My attitude? Lady, there ain't no attitude from me.'

Jamille kept her back to him, phone pressed to her ear as she examined her nails.

'You trying to get my ass fired?' Reggie flipped open the plastic hatch that was there for parcels to be handed through. 'I said what are you—'

Jamille spun round and grabbed Reggie around the neck, her fingers gripping his throat like a vice. His face was pressed up to the plastic, eyes wide and petrified, as she held him tight. 'Now, I don't like coming on all heavy, honey, that's not the way I work. All my friend was asking for was to be allowed through to pick up her friend's belongings. A simple request.'

'What the hell you doin'?' he rasped. 'I ain't author-ized to let you in without ID.'

Jamille squeezed a little tighter and the young guy screwed up his eyes. 'Reggie, I now have your name, and the street where you live. You understand where I'm coming from? So stop being so officious and just let us in.'

Reggie shook his head. 'Please . . . I can't . . . I'm going to college. I need this job. I'm a good kid.'

'Then do the right thing, Reggie. Let us in. And no funny business. Got it?'

'Okay . . . okay.' His eyes were watering. 'We're cool.'

Jamille released her grip. 'There's a good boy.'

Reggie pressed a buzzer, opening a side door that led into a cavernous metallic warehouse full of hundreds of lockers of different sizes. They headed down the first aisle, then spotted a sign for 61–70. Locker 62 was at eye level.

'What the hell were you doing, Jamille?' Deborah asked. 'That was downright brutal what you did to that guy.'

'That ain't brutal, honey. That was a choke hold I learned in judo class.'

'But the guy was just doing his job.'

'Yeah, whatever. Just open up the goddamn locker, Deborah, so we can get the hell out of here.'

Deborah took a deep breath before entering the code. There was a click and she pulled open the locker. Inside was a battered blue Nike backpack. She unzipped it to find a plastic protective folder that contained the documents. She didn't check the contents. That could wait until she and Jamille were safely back at the apartment.

'So, what've you got here?' Jamille said as Deborah unzipped the transparent plastic folder.

Deborah stared at the front page of a Congressional dossier. Below that there was a CIA report, the familiar seal with the bald eagle against a blue background at the top. 'The woman at MIT who taught John Hudson mentioned that he was obsessed with the twenty-eight missing pages in the Congressional Report into the September 11 attacks. This must be it.'

'No wonder they wanted to keep this quiet,' Deborah said eventually. 'This is dynamite.' She whistled. 'They're identifying a Saudi princess who runs some Islamic charities here in the States as one of the main backers of the September 11 attacks!'

'Shit!'

'I read the original report cover to cover. Came in at eight hundred-plus pages. Caused quite a storm at the time because people were well aware that no one wanted to mention the fact that members of the Saudi royal family were funding Al-Qaeda. We want their oil, they want our military hardware. Very cozy.'

Jamille pointed to the top of the page. 'Does this name mean anything to you?'

'Omar al-Bayoumi. Sure. Apparently he was living on the West Coast just before September 11. He was employed by the Saudi Civil Aviation Authority. He was based in San Diego and met two of the 9/11 terrorists in Los Angeles. They lived right across the street from him. He gave them money. Allegedly! Bit of a coincidence, right? There was a massive investigation by the feds, and the guy was cleared.'

'Princess Hind al-Bassi.' Jamille pointed to another name.

'She's the one. We need to find out everything about her,' Deborah said.

'That Hudson boy's death was no accident, Deborah, was it?'

'Never in a million years. Look, it says here that Islamic Health Centers she funded ended up giving money to some of the September 11 attackers. Apparently the princess has several homes in America, including one in Palm Beach. We've got a Florida connection.'

'So, what've we got here?' Jamille said, examining the CIA report. She read the title aloud. 'A Fallback Position – an Unacknowledged Special-Access Program (SAP) – entering discussions with Al-Qaeda.'

It took them about half an hour to read through all the information.

Deborah shook her head. 'This is mind-blowing. The CIA has a secret plan to enter into discussions with Al-Qaeda if a military solution can't be found. I'm going to courier all this to Harry Donovan.'

Jamille raised her eyebrows. 'Is that wise?'

'We can't keep this secret any longer.'

33

Deborah sat at her laptop for the next six hours. She Googled Princess Hind al-Bassi. She also accessed the *Miami Herald*'s vast archives and put in a call to Sam's old friend McNally. Slowly but surely a picture began to emerge. The princess was a reclusive super-rich woman who lived in Palm Beach, surrounded by a coterie of servants and advisers, in a palatial white marble mansion that had been built three years earlier, costing a cool twenty-six million dollars. Her nearest neighbors – about a mile from her fifty-acre estate – included Donald Trump and a former member of Led Zeppelin.

It was clear that she had channeled money through the 9/11 attackers but, amazingly, had not answered one single question about her involvement, according to secret FBI documents obtained by McNally from a source on Capitol Hill. On eight separate occasions the FBI had taken her in for questioning but had released her without charge. A leading FBI investigator concluded in a report that she was being 'protected by people on high'.

It emerged that the princess was the sister of the Saudi oil minister, no less, who himself was the eldest son of the current king. And she was highly educated. After Downe House, an exclusive all-girl boarding school in Berkshire, England, she had studied art history at Oxford. And then she'd moved to the States, to do a Master's in medieval art at Princeton.

She had remained single but, like the majority of people in Saudi Arabia, she adhered to Wahhabism, the strict theological interpretation of the Koran.

She was aged thirty-five. For the last eight years she had set up a variety of Islamic health projects in the States, but she'd also funded, according to the missing twenty-eight pages, at least two of the 9/11 attackers to the tune of nearly two hundred thousand US dollars. And she had underwritten the cost of building Islamic religious schools – madrassas – in Pakistan. Many of the Taliban were educated in such Saudi-financed schools. She had also contributed funds to build mosques in North Africa – including Morocco, Algeria and Tunisia – which were known to support Jihadists for operations in Iraq and Afghanistan. But her first foray into funding the madrassas in Afghanistan started way back in the 1980s, when she was at college in England. From these Islamic schools a wave of young Muslim men emerged who, tacitly backed by CIA dollars, were organized to fight first the Soviet Union – before they turned their attention to the West.

Deborah remembered reading about a major fraud investigation into bribes involving a British systems manufacturer and the Saudi government which had to be scrapped because the Saudis had threatened to pull the plug on a multibillion-dollar fighter-plane order.

Deborah turned her attention to the Simmons file. It wasn't long before she unearthed a little nugget of information. It transpired that Dr Simmons had apparently worked as a consultant for the Armed Forces Institute of Pathology. He had been assigned to look into the deaths of prisoners held by the CIA or their sub-contractors in Iraq and Afghanistan.

'How much do you wanna bet that Simmons was asked to go up to New York and do the autopsy?' Deborah said. 'Above the head of the local Chief Medical Examiner? The Armed Forces Institute of Pathology is an agency of the Department of Defense. Their HQ is based in Washington.'

Jamille shook her head.

'You know what the problem is, Jamille? There is just so much information that I don't know where to begin. There are two separate stories – perhaps three, if we consider Simmons.'

Her cellphone rang and she picked up. 'Deborah Jones,' she said, rolling her eyes at Jamille. 'Sure, Harry, I'll be there in half an hour.'

The remnants of a pale pink Biscayne sunset filtered through the conference-room blinds. Deborah felt strangely nervous as she sat across the table from the *Herald*'s executive editor.

Harry adjusted the large knot in his paisley-pattern tie. 'Have you lost your mind, Deborah? Well, have you? Aren't you on indefinite compassionate leave?'

Deborah shifted in her seat.

Harry put on his half-moon spectacles and flicked through the copies of the papers that had been couriered to him earlier by Deborah. 'Correct me if I'm wrong, but I was under the impression that your investigation into the deaths of John Hudson and Richard Turner had been shelved. I'm at a loss to understand this. I've watched your meteoric rise, Deborah, and I've never, ever had any problems with it. But I take the responsibilities that come with being executive editor at a major American newspaper very seriously and I'm damned if I will allow you to disregard the paper's line, whether you are Sam's girlfriend or not.'

'I don't like your tone, Harry. And I can't believe what I'm hearing. This is the breakthrough we've been looking for. It's a monumental story.'

'Who else knows about these documents?'

'Just us. And, of course, Michelle Turner, plus her friend in Miami. As far as I know, Michelle's gone underground.'

'Juan's gonna crucify you and Sam for this. You realize that. He's back in three days.'

'We got the story, Harry.'

'Deborah, why didn't you just let it lie?'

'For Christ's sake, Harry, if these papers are genuine, we have the story of the goddamn year. Of the decade.'

'It says here, in black and white, that the autopsy report on Richard Turner was carried out by Doctor Ken Meiter, a medical examiner in Brooklyn.'

'That has been contradicted by two separate sources.'

'You're starting to make it sound like a goddamn conspiracy.'

'Simmons has denied doing the autopsy, but we've found that he's a consultant for the Armed Forces Institute of Pathology, which does autopsies on prisoners who have died in CIA custody.'

Harry cleared his throat. 'These documents are alleged to have been printed out by Richard Turner in New York, right?'

'So we're led to believe.'

'But his sister had been given a copy – am I right? – for safekeeping?'

'Right.'

'I can't disagree with you, Deborah. This looks like one hell of a story. But my problem is with the CIA memo. How do we know it's genuine? Who the fuck's going to authenticate it?'

'There was a piece in *Time* by Seymour Hersh on a clandestine special forces group, assembled a few months after September 11,' Deborah said. 'Do you remember? The idea was to take out high-value Al-Qaeda operatives, bypassing all the diplomatic and legal niceties. That was set up as an unacknowledged special-access program, so only a handful of people within the Pentagon – and within the White House – knew about it.'

'The main question is,' Harry mused, 'is the government linked to these deaths?'

'Perhaps elements of the government,' Deborah said. 'But the truth is that we just don't know at this stage.'

'You still haven't answered my question. Who's going to authenticate?'

'I looked at the list of people who were on the Joint Inquiry into the 9/11 attacks. Sam's sister, Lauren, used to work in the office of former Wyoming Senator Randolph Sorley many years ago. He was a member of the Joint Inquiry.'

Harry continued to flick through the documents.

'He is now teaching international law at the University of Miami. There were rumors that he was particularly unhappy about those censored pages.'

'Look, Deborah, you're a helluva journalist, but I'm sorry to say that this isn't going any further. End of story.'

'Harry, please . . .'

'As of now, with immediate effect, your security pass and password for the newsroom and the building have been invalidated.'

34

The pounding techno music pumping out across the bowling alley was giving Nathan Stone a headache. He hated bowling. It reminded him of the Middle America he loathed. Bowling shoes, customized bowling ball, the beer, the head-splitting music, and the fake bonhomie.

Sooner be dead.

Strike was decidedly upscale and family-friendly, not like some of the skanky dives he knew. It was located in the Dolphin Mall, just off the turnpike in the west of the city.

Monster-sized giant plasma screens showing sports channels above the thirty-four glow-in-the-dark lanes, retro leather banquettes where people sat and drank in between games. At the next table, a huge family of overweight affluent Latinos ate pizzas and slurped their Coke, high-fiving every pin that went over.

Nathan signaled a pretty Hispanic waitress across. 'Large Coke, please,' he said.

She nodded politely. 'Si, señor.'

He smiled through gritted teeth. He loathed the all-pervasive Hispanic influence across Miami. It was everywhere. Spanish-language papers, radio stations blaring out shitty Cuban music, the taco shops popping up everywhere, the Latino menus.

What the fuck was all that about?

A cry went up further down the dimly lit lanes. Another strike.

Nathan noticed the dress code. It seemed like it was the smart-casual crowd. Chinos, button-downs and loafers for the men, smart jeans and preppy sweatshirts for the women. He noticed everything.

He was dressed accordingly. Chinos, boat shoes and pale blue linen shirt, conservative dark blue sweater on top. He could have been anybody. And that was good.

Even the slight burn on his cheek and the mark on the side of his neck had been concealed with his buttoned-up shirt and discreet skin-tone creams. The wounds on his thigh were scabbing over, although he was still popping codeine tablets to kill the pain.

The waitress returned with his drink, placing it carefully in front of him. 'Thank you, señorita,' he said, flashing his best Middle America smile.

She didn't smile back, which made him smile even more.

Whatever, bitch.

The whole placc was like where the dying went to

pretend they were living. The intense concentration of the game, the boozy after-hours office party at the bowling alley – as if that would help you unwind. Shit, if you wanted to unwind, why not pop some Quaaludes and wash them down with a quart of rum? Man, now that was major-league unwind.

But these fuckers were genuinely so into it.

Nathan continued to watch, smiling, feeling his nerve ends twitching, wondering when his subjects would turn up.

All around was the detritus of humankind, playing out their days in air-conditioned malls, like consumer battery farms, being force-fed a sludge of sugar-rush drink and chilli dogs, and copious quantities of piss-poor Bud and Michelob.

What he wouldn't give for a cold bottle of Heineken at the Deuce bar in South Beach, Stones playing loud in the background, serious drinkers only.

'Excuse me, señor,' a middle-aged middle-class Hispanic man said, smiling down at him. 'We noticed you sitting by yourself. Would you like to join our game?'

'Hey, appreciate that, but I'm under doctor's orders to just take it real easy, you know what I'm saying, buddy?'

The Hispanic gave a respectful nod and shook his hand. Then he headed back to his group. 'You have a nice night.'

Nathan smiled serenely, but frankly he was so wired that he couldn't think straight. Then he caught sight of them.

An attractive young Latina lady and a good-looking boy.

Rebecca Sinez smiled at him as she passed and he smiled back, giving the boy a soft pat on the head.

35

The first thing Deborah did when she got back to her condo was to call the university's Office of Media Relations and ask to speak to Senator Sorley. Within fifteen minutes Sorley returned her call.

His voice was deep, his delivery slow and considered.

'I'm sorry to bother you so late,' Deborah said. 'We were hoping you could help us. I believe you were on the Joint Inquiry into the 9/11 attacks, in your capacity as a former member of the Senate Intelligence Committee.'

'That is correct.'

'My boss is Sam Goldberg, managing editor of the *Miami Herald*. He mentioned that his sister Lauren used to run your office back in Wyoming, many years ago.'

'Well, I'll be damned. Must be fifteen years ago, maybe more.'

'Sir, we're trying to authenticate some important

documents which have come into our possession. The missing twenty-eight pages of the Joint Inquiry which you were part of.'

Sorley said nothing.

'And we were wondering if you would be prepared . . .'

'You know, it's funny. I argued vehemently that it was in the public interest. But we all came under enormous pressure, mainly from the White House, to acquiesce on that point. As a general rule, I think we're far too secretive as a society.'

'So will you have a look? I'd really appreciate it.'

'Very well. Drop them off with my secretary. I'll pick them up tomorrow afternoon.'

Late the following day, exhausted after spending hours at Sam's bedside while he dozed, Deborah was checking her personal e-mails on her BlackBerry in the kitchen as Jamille drank some coffee, when her cellphone rang.

'Miss Jones, I'm sorry,' Sorley said, sounding as though he might be afraid of being overheard, 'but I don't think I'm going to be able to help you after all. I think I was a tad hasty yesterday. Really, I would like to help, but this was an independent bi-partisan commission and I think I would be flouting not only convention but everything we stood for by helping you. I hope you'll accept my apologies. Pass on my regards to Sam and his family.'

It was a twenty-minute drive to Sorley's plantation-style house on Segovia Street in Coral Gables.

Deborah pressed the buzzer and wondered if anyone would answer. A few seconds later the door opened. Standing before them was an elegant gray-haired man in a dark blue tie and white shirt. 'Mr Sorley, I'm sorry to bother you. I'm Deborah Jones.'

'I thought I'd made myself clear, Miss Jones.'

'Five minutes of your time. That's all I ask.'

Sorley pursed his lips, then ushered Deborah and Jamille inside. They followed him, walking on a highly polished hardwood floor into a huge living room in which two pastel yellow sofas faced each other. Sorley sat down and Deborah and Jamille followed suit.

'Sam told me you're one of the good guys,' Deborah said. 'A man of your word. That's why I'm at a loss to understand why you've changed your mind so quickly. All we're asking is for you to confirm, one way or the other.'

'How did you get hold of this?'

'It started with the death of a young man called John Hudson.'

'Where is Sam now?'

'In hospital. He was attacked a couple of nights ago.'

'My God.'

At that moment an attractive woman in her mid-to-late fifties appeared. She wore a smart black dress. She was holding a cellphone in her hand. 'Excuse me, Randolph,' she said. 'The Provost wants a quick word.'

'I have to take this,' Sorley said. 'I'm sorry. Some after-dinner fundraising function the university is organizing.' He took the phone from his wife and left the room.

Kathleen Sorley shook Deborah's hand. 'You work for Sam, am I right?'

'Deborah Jones. Investigations editor of the *Miami Herald*.'

'Lovely to meet you. I've read your work on this dreadful housing-projects scandal.'

Kathleen went over to the door and closed it softly. 'How is Sam?'

'He'll be okay.'

'I shouldn't really be telling you . . . but Randolph received a call a couple of hours ago. Someone made veiled threats about our daughter Catherine. She's had her problems, you can guess . . . She's an only child. We've done our best, but ever since she was sixteen . . . She got in with a fast crowd. We're at our wits' end. And now we discover that our phones are being monitored . . .'

36

The following morning, Deborah spent three long hours calling all the members of the Joint Inquiry, both Republicans and Democrats. No one would help. Some were downright rude. Most were just curt, citing national security.

Deborah sat in front of her laptop and stared at the screen. 'Sam always says that there's someone out there who can point you in the right direction, it's just a matter of finding the right person.'

'Wouldn't it be easier to dump those twenty-eight pages for the time being, and focus on the CIA protocol?' Jamille asked.

'I need to speak to someone who understands the inner workings of the CIA. Someone who has an inside track on their role in the War on Terror. Someone like Larry Coen.'

'Who's he?'

'Crime reporter. He has contacts inside the FBI and the CIA.'

'What if it gets back to Harry Donovan? Then you really will be in the deep doo-doo.'

'Jamille, what's the name of that bookstore? Remember, there was a big turn-out when Bill Clinton did a signing?'

'Books and Books on Aragon Avenue. Why?'

'Didn't Faith tell us that she got a signed copy there, from some guy in intelligence? A specialist on the Taliban.'

Jamille called Faith, who gave her the name of Robert Sommers, once one of the CIA's foremost experts on Osama bin Laden. She then called McNally, who rang back an hour later with an address in the pretty Gulf Coast town of Dunedin, plus phone and cellphone numbers.

'So give the guy a call,' Jamille said, arms folded.

'That's not the way Sam would've done it. He once told me that it's harder to shut the door in someone's face than it is to hang up the phone.'

'How long do you reckon it takes to get to Dunedin?'

'Four hours, maybe a bit more. It's asking a bit much of you.'

'I'm a student, remember? I've got time to kill. Besides, I'm one of the smart ones. I saved every dime I ever earned.'

'Clever girl.'

'So, you want me to come with you?'

'Damn right. Let's do it.'

* * *

The drive up the west coast of Florida on I-75 North, past Naples to Dunedin, near Clearwater, a quaint small town with nearly forty thousand inhabitants, was a breeze – radio on, Doobie Brothers and Al Stewart classics playing non-stop. The sun was low in the sky when they arrived. Main Street was thriving – boutiques, antique shops, arty restaurants and lots of cyclists.

Deborah negotiated a few tree-lined side streets before pulling up outside a pale blue Key West-style home overlooking the Gulf. A BMW convertible was in the drive.

As Jamille moved to open the passenger door, Deborah said, 'I appreciate all you're doing for me, Jamille, but I can take care of this, thanks. Shouldn't be too long.'

She rang the bell. After a longish wait, a gray-haired heavily tanned man opened the door. He wore a turquoise shirt, tan slacks and two-tone shoes.

'Deborah Jones of the *Miami Herald*.'

'I'm not expecting you, am I?'

'We were wondering if you could help us.'

Sommers's smile revealed a perfect set of teeth. 'Have you read my book, Miss Jones?'

'I'm sorry to say I haven't.'

'Look, I don't mean to be rude, but people don't usually turn up at my front door without an appointment.'

'If you could give me twenty minutes of your time, sir. Some important documents have come into our possession.'

'You'd better make it quick.'

Deborah followed Sommers down a huge hallway into a good-sized living room, which led to a book-lined study with a view of the water.

'Would you like a drink?' He motioned for her to sit.

'Iced tea, thank you.'

'You drive up from Miami this afternoon?' He raised a quizzical eyebrow.

'Yes, sir.'

Deborah's gaze wandered round the shelves. There was a lot of military history and political biography. Churchill, Roosevelt, a few books on the Kennedys, Castro, Begin, Gandhi, Margaret Thatcher, alongside books on the Middle East. On Sommers's desk, beside his laptop, was Craig Unger's seminal *House of Bush, House of Saud: The Secret Relationship Between the World's Two Most Powerful Dynasties*.

A couple of minutes later, Sommers returned with an iced tea for her and a glass of red wine for him. He sat down at his desk, placing the glass of wine beside him. 'So, what do you want to know?'

'I understand that your book is highly critical of the administration's counter-terrorism policy. And that you advised a secret CIA unit which was trying to hunt bin Laden since 1996.'

'You have done your homework.'

'We've unearthed this protocol—'

'Do you have it with you?'

'Thought that might be too risky.'

Sommers nodded.

'This protocol is an unacknowledged CIA special-access program, which reveals plans to talk to Al-Qaeda in the event of military failure.'

Sommers's face remained impassive.

'You don't seem surprised,' Deborah said.

'What exactly do you want to know?'

'We need to authenticate the document . . .'

'Tell me, Miss Jones, what do you know about Al-Qaeda?'

'Just what I read in the newspapers. They're an Islamic terrorist group which hates the West.'

'Allow me to let you in on a little secret, Miss Jones. There is no such thing as Al-Qaeda.' Sommers's penetrating blue eyes fixed on her. 'Does that surprise you?'

'I thought—'

'Let me explain. Since 9/11, it has suited the purposes of the military-industrial complex, which benefits enormously from waging war, to have us believe that bin Laden is the devil. The literal translation of Al-Qaeda means "database".'

'I had no idea.'

'The database refers to the computer file that lists thousands of mujahadeen whom we armed and trained to help us defeat the Soviet Union. The operation was funded by the Saudis. One of the first people who alerted the world to this was the former British Foreign Secretary. Less than a month later, he was dead. Had a heart attack up a remote Scottish mountain.'

'What are you saying?'

'I'm saying, this is dangerous territory you're straying into. Al-Qaeda is not an international alliance of Islamic terrorism groups. For example, that terrorist attack in Indonesia, which the authorities claimed was the work of Al-Qaeda, was no such thing.'

'A convenient bogeyman.'

'Tell me this: why the hell haven't we tracked down bin Laden and killed the son of a bitch? I'll tell you why. He comes from a super-wealthy Saudi family, whose tentacles reach to the highest echelons of the Saudi elite, and into Big Oil, and into the pockets of American politicians. But most important, he was doing our dirty work in the 1980s. The CIA was giving military assistance to other guys like him in Afghanistan. He was on the database. It was a crazy decision which we'll rue for decades. All because of the imagined threat of the Russians and Communism.'

Deborah nodded.

'I've been saying this for years. But for some reason it didn't occur to anyone that these Islamic fascists would turn the Afghanistan thing into a jihad against the West, in particular against America. These same guys, backed by the CIA, then headed into Kosovo and Bosnia in the 1990s to take on the Serbs. We were happy. The Serbs were allies of the Russians, and we wanted, in geopolitical terms, to destroy Yugoslavia. Then there was Chechnya, a proxy war that we were running, against the old enemy – the Evil Empire.' Sommers laughed bitterly.

'I believe you also used to run the Counter-terroist Center's Islamic Extremist Branch, is that right? And set up the bin Laden issue station in 1996.'

Sommers shifted in his seat. 'Listen, if you're right, and the CIA is drawing up plans to talk to Al-Qaeda, then it's not only dumb – how can you reason with such people? – but also a monumental strategic blunder. The whole thing is a myth perpetrated by the West. What we're facing, in reality, is a patchwork of regional Islamic terrorist groups. But, having said that, there's no denying the civilized world is now in a fight to the death with these medieval crazies.'

'Who would have drawn up such a protocol?'

'It would have had to come from the top. The director. Michael Cunningham.'

'Do you still have contacts within the agency?'

Sommers drank some wine. 'A few.'

'And you haven't heard anything about this protocol.'

'Nope.'

'Does it seem credible?'

'Nothing would surprise me anymore. Tell you what, I can make a few calls and see what I come up with.'

'That would be terrific.'

Sommers laughed. 'Most of them think I'm nuts. The unit was known as the Manson Family, you know. We set off alarm bells everywhere. But what puzzles me is that I know most of the major players within the agency – and I haven't heard a whiff of this.'

'A young man drowned in the Everglades. We think

he had hacked into some computer or smartphone. And he unearthed not only the protocol, but the missing twenty-eight pages of the 9/11 Report. The publisher of the *Miami Herald* also received a call from a member of the intelligence community, asking him to drop the story. Because of the threat to national security.'

Sommers whistled softly. 'Tell me, does the name John Deutch mean anything to you, Miss Jones?'

Deborah shook her head.

'He was the director of the CIA in the mid-1990s. He was found to have classified material on unclassified laptops. There was a huge shitstorm. Now, nearly a dozen years later, some senior CIA guy's smartphone is hacked – and here we go again. You'd have thought they would've learned their lesson.'

37

The gentle breeze coming off Biscayne was welcome to Harry Donovan as he stood on a packed terrace at Vizcaya while sipping a glass of Cristal. In the background a quartet was playing Bartok. It was the annual $500-a-head Miami AIDS fundraiser at the huge mansion overlooking the bay. The coolest ticket in town. But only the smartest, wealthiest and most vulgar were invited.

It was excruciatingly fashionable. But it was one of the most important dates on his wife's social calendar, and he had to go. No ifs or buts.

Jacqueline sidled up to him, seeing he was bored.

'Why don't you mingle, Harry?'

'I don't want to mingle. I'm not in the mood. Thanks.'

'You seem distracted tonight, honey. Are you okay?'

Harry gazed off at the twinkling lights in the distance. 'Thinking of Sam, I guess.'

'What's the latest?'

'As of fifteen minutes ago? No damage, apart from recurring headaches and slight dizziness.'

Jacqueline clutched her chest rather theatrically. 'Poor Sam.'

'Sam's an old warhorse. He'll be fine.'

Harry had kept her in the dark about the associated threats made against him. He was glad to see the back of his wife, who soon decided it was time to do a bit more mingling. Then he found himself stuck with a sanctimonious tax expert who was based mostly in the Caymans and who wanted to discuss write-offs available to those who gave to certain good causes.

Harry's cellphone ringing saved him from more torture.

'Donovan,' he said, taking a sip of the champagne as he edged away from the throng.

'This won't take long.'

'Who's this?'

'That's not your concern. But you are *my* concern.'

Harry felt his stomach knot. It was a different voice than before. Smarter. Educated.

'I want to level with you. I'd like to apologize for what happened to your managing editor. That wasn't planned, I can assure you.'

'Who the hell are you?'

'I'll do the talking if you don't mind. I work for the government. Our contractor felt he had no choice when he was disturbed by Mr Goldberg. But I'm genuinely glad to hear he is on the mend.'

Harry said nothing as the laughter and music filtered down to him.

'Moreover, we are greatly encouraged by your move to stop Miss Jones entering the *Herald*'s offices. A masterstroke, if I may say so.'

'How the hell do you know that?'

'We know a lot of things. But, I'm sorry to say, we are concerned that Miss Jones isn't letting up with her obsession. Now, we have tried to be reasonable—'

'You have to be kidding!'

'Please don't interrupt, Mr Donovan. I have nothing but admiration for you. The way you have worked so hard at climbing the newspaper ladder as well as the social ladder. Black tie suits you.'

Harry looked around, wondering how the hell the unseen man knew.

'High-definition images, if you want to know. And I've read your file.'

'What file?'

The man laughed. '"What file?" Everyone has a file. I have yours on my desk as we speak.'

Harry stayed quiet.

'You've got some secrets, that's for sure, Harry.' There was an icy edge to the man's voice now. 'But who hasn't?'

'What exactly do you want?'

'You have the final say if a story ends up in the *Herald*. And that's why we were so delighted to find out about your dalliance with the awfully attractive Ms Sinez. And the son? That was a rare bonus, ensuring you stay compliant. But what concerns me is your approach to Michael Cunningham. That was just plain dumb.'

'I was told not to contact the cops.'

'You don't contact *anyone*. Do you understand me?'

Harry didn't reply.

'And those documents sent to you by Deborah Jones, purporting to show some Saudi links and a CIA protocol. We have already taken the precaution of removing them from your office safe.'

'What?'

'So just forget all about it, okay?'

'Is it genuine?'

'It's bullshit. But that's none of your concern. Appearances are everything. In the wrong hands, naive hands . . . we do not need a diplomatic incident.'

'Are you finished?'

'Not quite. There's something else. We didn't realize until we examined your file that you had a special arrangement, way back, with Michael Cunningham. A deal brokered by your wife.'

Harry signaled to Jacqueline on the terrace that he'd be right with her.

'You thought that, when you met up, it was simply a verbal arrangement. He put a scenario to you, and you accepted. No one knew apart from you two – and Jacqueline. That is, until now. You might've been contemplating leaving your wife and having the humiliation of your affair splashed across the press. But this is something else altogether, isn't it?'

Harry wondered if the man was bluffing. 'Look, this is all very interesting, but—'

'Harry, you're a man who obviously thinks of number one, and I respect that. I admire that. It's the American way. But, unfortunately, Cunningham has shafted you. The whole conversation at that stunning house of yours on Key Biscayne was bugged, from beginning to end. You want me to play you the tape?'

'What in God's name are you going on about?'

'He virtually guaranteed you the job. It was a shoo-in, he said. But I believe it was your wife's family who made the first move, arranging the whole meet. Mutual interest, so to speak.'

Harry said nothing.

'Don't make me use this. That's all I'm saying.'

38

Unable to sleep, Nathan Stone was staring at his reflection in the bathroom mirror, shadows under his sunken blue eyes. He focused on the huge curved scar on the right side of his shoulder. A street-gang fight back in New York, after school. Whites and spics. He had stood his ground as they'd swarmed all over him. He'd fought back, in spite of having his arm slashed to the bone. It was stupid, looking back. But he had managed to stab one little fucker in the side of the neck.

No one fucked with him after that day. They could see he didn't care. He had no fear. And he found out that was what really scared people.

He splashed cold water on his face, trying to wake himself up after sleeping for most of the day. Drying his face, he wondered how long the surveillance would continue.

Taking her out with a bullet in the head on I-75 as

he passed in his car would have been the best bet. It would have looked like just another senseless murder on the Florida freeway. But his handler didn't want it done that way, fearing eyewitnesses.

His instructions were simply to follow her, and report back.

Nathan went through to his bedroom and shut the blinds before switching on his laptop. Then he began to watch the footage of Deborah Jones that he'd filmed secretly from behind the privacy windows of his SUV as she'd worked out with her soccer team in Palmer Park a few days earlier.

He noticed that she pushed her body harder than any of the other girls. Sweat stains made a pattern on the back of her T-shirt.

His cellphone rang.

'Things are moving quite quickly now. We've switched to twenty-four/seven. Any back-up – listening devices, electronic tracking – you name it, you've got it.'

The following morning, Nathan Stone stood on the first-floor balcony of his no-star, men-only motel – the Sunshine Hotel – in Surfside, a small community ten minutes north of South Beach. He dragged on his cigarette as he watched an elderly gray-haired man in the pool below him swim a slow but powerful breaststroke as the sun rose in a burnt orange sky.

It was the crummiest motel in the area, and Nathan felt perfectly at home. No crying babies, no women to give him grief, just guys who couldn't afford to live or stay anywhere else. There was the usual collection of gays, but that didn't bother him like it used to.

They kept themselves to themselves, and that was just fine. And he didn't pay any bills. Nothing. No rent, no bar tab, no food bills: nothing. Everything was picked up by the man. If they needed to contact him, it was always through the cellphone or a message at the front desk, asking him to 'call head office', code for his handler at Langley.

The trip to Dunedin had taken a lot out of him. So too had New York. Bad memories resurfaced as soon as he set foot in the Lower East Side.

The thought of what he'd endured overwhelmed him occasionally, and he'd slug down bourbon until his father's face was blotted from his mind. But the next morning he'd always see his father's bloodshot eyes staring back at him out of the mirror as he shaved.

After Helen had been taken from him in the dead of night, all that was left was the army. He loved the harsh training, being screamed at. He crawled through mud and ran until he was sick. He learned how to fight. Pain didn't mean a thing to him.

They were assessing him the whole time. Aged twenty-two, Nathan Stone fit the psychological profile for a covert military unit. Was he interested?

Within the year, he was training Colombian troops in torture techniques, choke holds, professional interrogation methods including 'water boarding' – where a victim has water poured over their face to simulate drowning – and other specialties, including electric-shock treatment. But since 9/11 he'd been deployed at 'black sites' in Eastern Europe – classified, secret interrogation facilities, primarily in Poland and Romania – where high-value Al-Qaeda operatives were kept. Mock killings, actual killings, surveillance operations and assassinations. He worked wherever he was sent. He didn't care. And he didn't ask questions.

Even when people were pleading for their lives, Nathan Stone could blot it out. He saw the desperate look in their eyes, which he himself must've had as a child when his father was about to take his thick leather belt to him. But he just smiled back. Their screams were like background music.

He didn't care if they answered the question or not. Nathan Stone began to need the buzz that came from the fear he instilled in men, women and children.

His most recent jaunt abroad had been to the grimy basement of the Interior Ministry in Baghdad, where a Shia police unit, instructed by the Americans, was torturing Sunni prisoners. Sometimes he was driven in a blacked-out SUV around the worst slums to pick up suspects at random and take them back for interro-gation. It was part of a strategy to entrench fear in the psyche of the Iraqi people. It was nothing to do with liberation or democracy.

At Abu Ghraib, Stone was part of 'Copper Green', the code name given to a black-op program designed to physically harm and sexually humiliate Arab men. The object was to break their will, to make them more malleable.

Stone showed the Shia cops how to sodomize Arab boys with batons in front of their friends while photographing and videoing the whole thing. How to break a prisoner's leg by stamping repeatedly on it. He instructed military police and private contractors on techniques of pouring acid into the eyes of detainees. But the interrogators needed no advice on the technique of rape.

They were all only following orders.

Nathan Stone loved the freedom. He received a call; he did a job.

Back in his bleak room, he opened up his laptop and gazed at the infra-red pictures he'd taken of the young *Miami Herald* journalist – Deborah Jones – running screaming out of the warehouse in Brooklyn. And he smiled.

39

The cloying voice of Diane Sawyer as she interviewed Henry Kissinger on *Good Morning America* about the situation in Iraq roused Deborah from a deep sleep. She lay in bed for a few moments as the egregious questioning of Kissinger continued apace. Sawyer was treating the elder statesman with kid gloves. The man who escalated the Vietnam war. The man responsible for the illegal carpet-bombing of Laos and Cambodia. The man who advised President George W. Bush against a rapid withdrawal of coalition troops in Iraq. Now he had the audacity to declare that the war couldn't be won, and America would have to talk to regional power-brokers like Iran.

It was breathtaking. How could he be taken seriously? Why wasn't he behind bars?

Deborah heard Jamille talking on her cellphone in the living room. She showered and went through to the kitchen where a fresh pot of coffee, orange juice and a plate of croissants awaited.

'You sleep well?' Jamille asked, ending her call.

'Not too bad.'

'Heard you talking in your sleep. Shouting as well. Scared the shit out of me.'

'You mind turning that woman down? She's giving me a headache.'

Jamille reached for the remote control. 'Sorry.' Then she opened the blinds. 'Man, you never told me what the views were like up here.'

Deborah drank some juice and then took a large chunk out of a croissant. She noticed a plain white envelope, her name on it, lying on the sofa. 'What's that?'

'I found it this morning. Must've been pushed through the door last night.'

Deborah examined the elegant old-style handwriting. A fountain pen had been used. She opened up the seal and pulled out a small note. It was from Robert Sommers. Her heart began to pound hard.

It read:

I want to try and help you. We need to talk face to face. But I can't risk calling you or texting you. They're monitoring everything. Calls and e-mails. Maybe even close surveillance. Here's what I propose:

After you visit Sam at the hospital this morning, hop on the Metro at Civic Center at 10 a.m. precisely and head north. Bring copies of the protocol and missing pages with you. I'll be wearing a red Buccaneers hat. Don't be afraid. Robert S.

She handed the letter to Jamille.
'What do you think?' Deborah asked.
'Could be a set-up.'
Deborah reflected for a few moments. 'I need to do this. But I'll understand if you don't want to come along with me . . . Honestly, it's not a problem.'
'You're crazy, girl, you know that?' Jamille shook her head. 'You never give up, do you?'

At the hospital, it was a relief to see Sam sitting up in bed, and smiling. But he was still obviously very weak. Deborah kissed him on the cheek, then got a progress report from his doctor and his two sisters. She put on a brave smile. She didn't tell him about the note, or that her security pass had been withdrawn. She didn't want to worry him. When the visit was over, she leaned over and kissed him on the cheek, whispering in his ear, 'It's gonna be fine, honey. You get well. I love you.'

The Civic Center metrorail station was stifling hot and seething with hot, sweaty people. The station was situated at the intersection of Northwest 12th Avenue and 15th Street, and was popular with all those who worked in or visited the nearby Jackson Memorial Hospital, the Bascom Palmer Eye Institute, the Veterans Hospital and the Cedars Medical Center. But Deborah hadn't used it for years, preferring the privacy and safety of her car.

At 10.01 a.m. the train pulled up and Deborah found a window seat, Jamille beside her. The documents were in the small rucksack that Jamille was carrying.

Sommers got on at the next stop, the Santa Clara station. He was wearing shades and a distinctive red Tampa Buccaneers hat, a button-down white shirt, chinos and brown moccasins. He sat down in the seat behind them.

'Glad you made it.' He didn't waste any time. 'You got the documents?'

Jamille took off the rucksack and handed it over. Sommers rummaged inside and pulled out the documents. He removed his dark glasses, scanning the pages feverishly. Every time the train stopped at a station Deborah looked around anxiously, half-expecting to see the man with the crazy dark eyes who'd attacked her and Sam.

But gradually she relaxed. Sommers continued reading on, all the way to Palmetto. The color drained from his face.

'All this came from your hacker?'

'We believe so,' Deborah replied. 'This was a hard copy made by a friend of his, who has also wound up dead.'

'Sounds like the NCS.'

'Who the hell are they?'

'National Clandestine Service. Covert action, human-intelligence gathering, right. They had to be overhauled after 9/11. After a few too many mistakes.' Sommers placed the documents back in the rucksack and handed it to Jamille. 'It's complete capitulation.'

'So, who would have drawn it up?'

'You told me that the *Herald*'s publisher was warned off this story because of national security, right?'

'I'm sorry to say that's true.'

'This has to be the work of Michael Cunningham.'

'The way I see it, we have two options. Firstly, we sit tight on what we've got.' There was a pause while the message sank in. 'Or we approach the CIA direct. This is their program, after all. Right, Robert?'

Sommers winced. 'Why would they acknowledge an unacknowledged program with some reporter? I've tried, and I'm on the inside. They'd set their lawyers on you, citing national security and all that crap.'

Deborah nodded.

'The CIA is a monster, Deborah. They can make your worst nightmares come true.'

'What do you know about Cunningham?'

'He gets handed files and information on everything from the analysis of an interrogation of a leading Islamacist to ongoing assassination plots by Mossad – you name it. He arrived after I left, so I don't know him personally. But the job can take over your life. You end up living in an alternative universe, populated by terrorists, potential terrorists and foreign spies. It's an impossible task.'

'So how am I going to get to him?'

Sommers put on his shades. 'My advice? Go through official channels. You may be lucky.'

* * *

Later that night, back in her condo with Jamille after spending most of the day and evening at Sam's bedside, Deborah punched in the number for Marion Main, Director of Media Relations for the CIA, on her BlackBerry. She waited for nearly a minute as it rang and rang.

'Marion Main. How can I help at this ungodly hour?'

'Sorry to bother you, Marion. Deborah Jones of the *Miami Herald*.'

'Do you know what time it is?'

'I'm sorry . . .' Deborah explained that she had 'sensitive' documents in her possession. And that the paper urgently needed to authenticate what they had, preferably with the Director. She gave her BlackBerry number and e-mail address.

'I'm not promising anything, but I'll see what I can do,' Marion said.

Just before midnight, she called back. 'If you want to arrange an interview at a later date,' she said, 'he'd be delighted to help you in any way he can.'

'I'm just asking for a few minutes of his time. How about tomorrow?'

'That just not possible right now. It's been a long day. I'm sorry.'

40

Just after one in the morning, Nathan Stone noticed the smirk on the concierge's face as his *jinetera*, a Cuban prostitute he'd known for years who was wearing a short red leather skirt and tight white crop-top, pretended to stumble on her way out of the Hyatt and into the steamy Miami night, a middle-aged man on her arm. The man's other hand was up her skirt.

Nathan had asked Rosa, a seventeen-year-old who'd escaped the Havana slums as a child prostitute, to hang around the hotel's lobby bar for an hour. Within five minutes of arriving she began flirting with the middle-aged white guy who was sinking beers by himself. A short while later she'd called Nathan from inside the hotel's Alcazaba nightclub as the man ordered more drinks at the bar. Nathan didn't tell her the man's name. But she was playing her part perfectly.

He followed them from a distance, careful to stay in

the shadows at least fifty yards behind. Rosa led him two blocks to the bustling Miracle Mile, a four-block district of restaurants, art galleries, fancy boutiques and live theaters. It ran along Coral Way between LeJeune and Douglas.

Nathan lit a cigarette as the crowds thickened and he felt his heart begin to beat that bit faster as he kept his eyes locked on to the couple. He was in his element, crazy thoughts tearing through his head. The steroids and speed had kicked in.

Down Salzedo they went and along Andalusia Avenue to an Irish bar. They stayed for twenty minutes. Then Rosa and the man staggered half a dozen blocks to the trendy Globe Bar on Alhambra. People were spilling out onto the street, hanging on to their drinks, while the Latin dance tunes pumped out hard. No one gave the couple a second glance as they headed inside.

Nathan remained in the shadows, occasionally glancing at his watch. He reflected how pathetic men were when easy women were presented to them on a plate.

Apparently the man had a long-term girlfriend, a Linda Shoulton. She worked as a partner in a high-powered private equity firm, Groschman Capital Management, in midtown Manhattan during the week, and would head back to Dunedin at the weekends.

Just before two a.m. Rosa emerged through the throng outside the bar. She was alone. She walked back towards the Miracle Mile, never glancing in Nathan's direction. He walked off the other way.

Less than a minute later, his cellphone rang with a text message that contained a picture of the man – Robert Sommers – lying semi-naked with Rosa on the floor of the bar's toilet. It was not a great snap, taken at arm's length by the Cuban girl, but it did the business.

A short while later Nathan's cellphone rang again. 'You get it?'

'Very good, Rosa. Where is he now?'

'Out of it.'

'I assume you slipped him the mickey?'

'Chloral hydrate in his bottle of Schlitz, as requested. By the way, mister, you owe me one thousand dollars.'

'It's already in your mother's account, Rosa. I'll be in touch.'

Nathan ended the call and sent the picture to the cellphone of his handler, then on to Linda Shoulton, with the short message, 'When the cat's away, the mice will play.'

He couldn't keep the grin off his face as he headed into the night.

41

Deborah awoke in a cold sweat as the early-morning light flooded her bedroom. Her phone was ringing.

'We need to talk, Deborah.' It was Sommers. 'I've just had the *National Enquirer* on the phone. They have been sent a photo of me with a girl I bumped into at the Hyatt last night. I've been set up.'

'But why?'

'Don't you get it? This is a warning shot, not to get involved with you. My girlfriend's been sent the picture too. It's even on the fucking Internet. I'm meeting my lawyer downtown in an hour,' Sommers continued. 'I just wanted you to know what had happened . . .'

The news from Sommers unsettled Deborah. They meant business, whoever they were, but she was undeterred. Half an hour later she had come up with a name which kept recurring in Internet searches of academics who specialized in the workings of the CIA. She printed out a couple of profiles from *Time* and *Newsweek* and showed them to Jamille.

'Professor Norman McCabe of Yale. You heard of this guy?'

'Means nothing to me.'

'He's been a thorn in the side of the CIA since Vietnam. Everything from the CIA's links with heroin cartels in Southeast Asia to the torture chambers at Abu Ghraib. He's got to be worth a try.'

'But what's he going to tell you that Sommers couldn't? He's not inside track. Also, he may not appreciate being drawn into this investigation after what happened to Sorley and Sommers.'

'Someone apart from me has to be interested in the truth.'

'I'm starting to get a bad feeling about this, honey.'

McCabe answered the phone immediately.

'Deborah Jones of the *Miami Herald*. Can you spare a few minutes?'

'The last time a journalist asked me that, I was on the phone for nearly two hours.'

Deborah laughed. 'I assure you, sir, ten minutes tops.'

'Okay, how can I help?'

Deborah went over the story again. 'So, does this sound like a CIA operation to you?'

'The Agency is a law unto itself,' McCabe said. 'Your

story puts me in mind of the Iran-Contra arms-for-hostages operation, which was masterminded by Bill Casey, the CIA's director during the Reagan years. They financed the Contras from arms sales to Iran. The hallmarks of that operation were, according to the Senate House Investigating Committee, secrecy, deception and disdain for the law.'

'So do you think it's possible that the CIA, or some cabal within Langley, could be involved in the deaths of John Hudson and Richard Turner?'

'You've described a classic pattern of events. Tell me, Miss Jones, does the name Lieutenant Colonel Daniel Martin mean anything to you?'

'No.'

'In 1964 he was asked by the CIA to terminate the life of Bruce William Pitzer. Martin refused as the assassination was to be on American soil. The following year Mr Pitzer was found dead in his office. It was recorded as suicide.'

'What's your point?'

'My point, Miss Jones,' McCabe said, as if running out of patience, 'is this. Do you know what Bruce William Pitzer did for a living?'

'No.'

'He was a photo technician, present during the autopsy of John F. Kennedy at Bethesda Naval Hospital, Maryland.'

'Are you saying there are parallels?'

'Absolutely. Whilst you may have struck gold in

journalistic terms, you've also saddled yourself with a major problem. You might be better off forgetting the whole thing.'

'I haven't come this far to give up now.'

'Well, I wish you good luck, Miss Jones, and I admire your courage and persistence. Remember – the CIA, oil, big business, dictators, and Central and South American death squads are all one and the same thing. Whatever they tell you, don't believe a word. Now, if that's all, I've got a tutorial in five minutes to prepare for. Nice talking to you.'

42

The hours dragged on, but by mid-afternoon Marion Main had still failed to get back to Deborah.

'McCabe,' Deborah said eventually, snapping her fingers. She felt a fool for not asking him before. 'Goddamn, he's got to be worth a try.'

Jamille rolled her eyes. 'You called him this morning. Besides, he's not going to give you Cunningham's cellphone number, honey, is he? Get real.'

'The professor was very amenable. Gotta be worth a shot. He just might have the number.'

'Yeah, but he's not gonna divulge that to you, is he?'

'Why not?'

'What you been smoking, honey? You're gonna call him up again and say, "Gee, Professor McCabe, you don't happen to have Michael Cunningham's cellphone number handy, do you?" It ain't gonna happen. Just sit tight and wait for that CIA bitch to get back to you. Plus, he ain't a fan of the CIA, is he?'

'No harm in trying. Besides, it might be doomsday before Marion Main gets back to me.' Deborah dialed McCabe's number and waited.

'You're crazy, you do know that?' Jamille said.

Deborah shrugged.

McCabe came on the line sounding flustered, but to Deborah's surprise he casually gave out the number, stressing that she 'shouldn't divulge under any circumstances' where she had got it from.

'I owe you one, professor,' she said, and put down the phone. Then she looked across at Jamille and grinned. 'You were saying, honey?'

'Not another word,' Jamille said, trying hard to suppress a smile.

Although she was excited at the breakthrough, Deborah still felt distinctly uneasy. Sure, she could just call the number. But first she wanted to run the idea by Sam.

She had to wait until Sam's sisters left his bedside to grab a coffee before she could outline her plan of action.

He didn't raise any objections, maybe because he was only half awake.

Half an hour later, in her condo, Deborah made the call from her cellphone.

Amazingly, Michael Cunningham picked up.

'Good afternoon, sir. My name is Deborah Jones of the *Miami Herald*. I believe you know our executive editor, Harry Donovan. We did a profile of you a little while back.'

'I know Harry. But I think you'd be better advised to follow procedural guidelines, young lady, and contact our press people.'

'The matter is a rather delicate one, sir. Documents have come into our possession. And it is vital to establish their authenticity.'

'I don't have time for this. Speak to Marion Main.'

'I've tried that already. She wanted to line up an interview when you returned. We need to speak to you now.'

'I'm sorry, Miss Jones. Everything goes through Marion. Don't use this number again.'

Cunningham hung up.

'What are we going to do now?' Jamille asked Deborah.

'What the man said. Speak to Marion Main, and put some pressure on her as well.'

'What kind of pressure?'

'You'll see.'

Marion Main answered at the third ring.

'Marion, hi, Deborah Jones again.'

'It's not still about these goddamn documents, is it?'

'I've just spoken to the director.'

A long silence ensued. 'I beg your pardon?'

'And he's referring us back to you.'

'How on God's earth did you get his number?'

Deborah ignored the question. 'Look, we're going through official channels as he's requested we do, and we just want him to answer some specific questions about papers we have. Otherwise we will have no choice but to run with this story as it stands.'

'Unbelievable. You guys are the limit. You've gone behind my back and approached the director on his private number. I've got a good mind to take this up with Harry Donovan.'

Deborah looked across at Jamille who smiled back at her. 'He's sitting right here,' she lied. 'Do you want to speak to him?'

'That won't be necessary. I'm going to put in an urgent media request call on your behalf. I can't promise anything. But leave it with me till four p.m.'

By five o'clock Deborah hadn't heard anything. Resigned to not getting the call, her luck suddenly changed when the phone rang. It was Marion Main.

'Sorry about the delay. Mr Cunningham is simply too busy at the moment. But he has given you the go-ahead to talk to his deputy. How does that sound?'

'I need to speak to the guy at the top.'

'The Deputy Director is willing to speak to you frankly on his secure line. But only for five minutes. Take it or leave it.'

'I'll take it. Thank you, Marion. I appreciate your help.'

Deborah got straight through to Cunningham's deputy who was clearly expecting her call.

'Right. This is how it's going to work.' He sounded crisp and efficient. 'I am going to give you a heads-up on this. But we must set out the ground rules before I take you into my confidence. First of all, what I'm going to tell you cannot go in the paper. Is that clear?'

'You got it.'

'We have reason to believe that a low-ranking CIA official has fabricated documents to make it look as if they are authentic CIA programs. Classic black ops.'

'So how does John Hudson fit into this?'

'I don't want to go into too much detail, but I can tell you that he was recruited by this CIA man to provide cover for his internal spying operation.'

'So are you saying that what we have here is a complete fabrication designed to undermine American national security?'

'Exactly. We have a spy in our midst.'

Deborah's mind was racing.

'But it wouldn't be the first time in modern history,' he said, 'that such things have happened. Have you ever heard of the Zinoviev Letter?'

'I've heard of it . . .'

'Way back in 1924, MI5 in Britain claimed they'd intercepted a letter written by Grigory Zinoviev, chairman of the Comintern in the Soviet Union.'

'What has this got to do with the papers we have?'

'In his letter, Zinoviev urged British communists to promote revolution through acts of sedition. MI5 claimed that the letter was genuine. And it was shown to the Labour Prime Minister. He agreed that the letter should be kept secret, but someone leaked it to the newspapers. It was published before the 1924 election, contributing to the defeat of the Labour Party.'

'So you are saying the *Miami Herald* is being manipulated, just like John Hudson was.'

'Almost certainly. We are convinced that Hudson was being used as a pawn in a very elaborate scheme.'

'And where is this CIA man now?'

'I cannot comment on that.'

Deborah said nothing.

'Well, if that's everything Miss Jones. As I said, everything we've discussed must remain strictly confidential. We cannot risk jeopardizing the ongoing operation. Is that understood?'

'I appreciate your candor, sir. Thank you.'

'So, what do you think?' Jamille said, after Deborah had relayed the gist of the story.

'I don't know what to believe anymore.'

43

The late-night air was sticky and a wind was whipping across the Rickenbacker causeway, as Harry Donovan drove home. He had just endured a fourteen-hour shift and hadn't slept properly in days. Increasingly he wondered if he wasn't being watched. And all the while he was consumed by dread.

When he got home he was surprised to see that all the lights were on.

'Hey, honey,' he shouted, as he shut the front door. His voice echoed around the high cathedral ceiling. 'Weren't you supposed to be at Rosie O'Donnell's party tonight?'

No answer.

Harry opened the French doors and went out onto the terrace. His wife sat gazing out over the pool and swaying palms below, a glass of white wine in her hand. 'There you are,' he said. 'I was saying, weren't you—'

'I cancelled.'

Harry took a few moments to compose himself. 'Cancelled? You never cancel. Are you feeling okay?'

Jackie turned to face him. He could see she'd been crying. 'What do you take me for, Harry?'

In that terrible moment, he knew that she knew.

Harry slumped in a seat opposite her.

'Are you insane?' she hissed.

Harry felt sick and put his head in his hands. 'Please, I can explain—'

'Explain? You wanna explain the little note delivered by courier, along with half a dozen twelve-by-eight color pictures of you and your son? They're upstairs if you want to check.'

Harry closed his eyes.

'I know you've not had feelings for me, Harry, for quite some time. I understand that. But this is, to say the least, is . . .' She didn't finish the sentence. Instead, she knocked back her drink before smashing the glass onto the clay-tiled terrace. 'I feel as if I'm going insane,' she snapped.

Harry nodded and held out his hand. She brushed it away.

'How *could* you, Harry? Am I a figure of fun for you?'

'Jackie, please listen to me.'

She stood up, arms folded, shaking her head. 'No, you

listen to me. I want to know how this happened. I mean . . . I mean she was a fucking *kid*, Harry. She was your secretary. What the hell were you thinking? It's pathetic.'

'I know it's pathetic. I'm not denying that. But it happened. I was drunk. I messed up. And I have a child. A boy who needs me.'

'Well, that's just great. How lovely for you and your Latina mistress.'

'She isn't my mistress. It was just one night.'

Jackie snorted. 'I want answers. And I want them right now. Why is this happening? What the hell is going on?'

'In a word, blackmail.'

The color drained from her face. 'Tell me everything. Tell me about the affair. Tell me about the boy. That's all I want to hear. And no more lies. I'm sick of lies.'

Harry took a deep breath. For the next ten minutes, Jackie listened in stunned silence, occasionally covering her mouth with her hand. When he finished, he just sat and waited for her response.

When Jackie spoke her voice was shaking. 'Do you love her?'

'I never loved her. I told you, it was a drunken one-night fling. I was an asshole.'

'Where does she live?'

'North end of Key Biscayne. Little condo.'

'What's the boy's name?

Harry sighed. 'Andrew Donovan.'

'School?'

'He attends Ransom Everglades, in the Grove.'

'Expensive. Harry, I never check what goes in or out. I trust you not to spend all our money. And it is *our* money, has been since we married.'

'I wasn't running away with your money. I was just wanting the best for my son.'

Jackie's eyes brimmed with tears. 'Is this because I didn't want children? Is that at the root of this?'

'No, it's just the way things happened. Look, I didn't mean for this to come out. I just wanted to forget it.'

Jackie bowed her head and sighed.

'There's something else.'

'What?'

'The guy who called the other night – he knew all about the little meeting that you arranged with Michael Cunningham before I became executive editor.'

'I don't believe it . . .'

'These people mean business, I tell you. And I don't know where it's going to end.'

'And where the hell is Juan while all this is going on?'

'Should be back tomorrow, maybe the day after.'

'Okay – this is how it's going to work. I know about the boy, and the relationship, and I'll have to deal with that. We will support him educationally, and buy the condo outright, and of course you must see him whenever you want. But never bring him over here, okay? He's not *my* son.'

'Of course.'

Jackie tilted her head back in the balmy breeze. 'Can you remember what you discussed with Michael at the meeting?'

'Of course. He was asking me all these geopolitical questions, my views on Israel, military spending plans, NASA, civil liberties arguments versus national security, a whole range of stuff.'

'And he liked what you said?'

'He told me that he wished me well in my career, and said he hoped I'd be appointed executive editor of one of the country's most important newspapers.'

'Yes, but did he specifically say that he'd try and pull some strings?'

'Not in so many words. He was careful not to give any assurances, but he did say that he would, and I'm quoting, "See what I can do." I wish to God I hadn't listened to you . . .'

'I was just trying to help you, for God's sake. Hindsight's a wonderful thing, Harry. But we are where we are. This is what I propose. Forget the cops, I wouldn't trust them as far as I could throw them. But the feds, they're something else.'

'I agree, Jackie. But if these guys find out, who the hell knows what will happen? Apparently our calls are being monitored, for chrissakes. I can't survive if this shit really hits the fan.'

'We have to deal with this. FBI office in North Miami Beach, just head straight there, no calls, nothing. Speak to Ron Martinez.'

'I can't right now. I'm flying to New York for the conference tomorrow – you know that. I can't miss it.'

'Can't you cancel?'

Harry shook his head.

'Make it the day after, then. The sooner this is sorted, the better.'

44

Nathan Stone's heart sank at the sight of the seven-storey monstrosity of the South Florida Evaluation and Treatment Center. He pulled up at the visitor's parking lot and, after being frisked by a surly black guard, he was escorted to a visitor's room by a ruddy-faced middle-aged white man, a rarity in Miami these days.

The place reeked of disinfectant, bad cooking and coffee.

Helen was sitting cross-legged on a seat. She stretched out her arms when Nathan walked in. 'My handsome big brother,' she said. 'My, you look smart.'

Nathan was wearing a sharp pale blue suit and black slip-on leather shoes.

'You have a date later, huh?'

Nathan leaned down to kiss his sister. She smelled of cigarette smoke and stale sweat. 'Yeah . . . I'm meeting a girl tonight. But I had to meet my number one girl first, right?'

His sister laughed and started fiddling with her hair. 'So, do you wanna tell me about her? Where did you meet?'

'In a bar. And we got chatting. Name's Rosa. She's from Cuba. Very pretty.'

'You got a picture?'

'We only just met. I promised I'd take her for a meal tonight.'

'Treat her nice, Nathan. Promise?'

'Of course.'

'Beautiful suit. Where did you get that?'

'Made-to-measure. Tony Rizzo's in Bal Harbor.'

'Well, if that doesn't do it for her I don't know what will.'

Nathan leaned over and held her hand. 'What about you?'

'What about me?'

'What've you been up to?'

'I've started art-therapy classes.'

'Hey, that's great. So, what do you paint?'

'Mostly pictures of you. Oil paintings.'

'Can I see them?'

'I've not really finished yet. But I will soon. You can hang them in your apartment in South Beach.'

Nathan had created a complete imaginary world for Helen, one in which her brother did real-estate deals, advised governments on social policy and had a box at Dolphin Stadium.

'Tell me more about Rosa.'

'Like what?'

'Like what she does for a living?'

'She works in real estate, too. High-end Miami condos. In fact, I'm thinking about investing in a new development at Wynwood.'

Helen smiled and gazed out of a window, at the barbed wire round the perimeter glistening in the sun. 'What does she look like?'

'Very pretty . . . Very religious.'

'Oh, that's good. I pray every day.'

'What do you pray for?'

'I pray that one day you meet the right girl. And maybe she'll visit me too. One day. That would be neat.'

Nathan looked into his sister's tired eyes and smiled. 'What have I always told you, Helen?'

'You'll never leave me.'

'I swear to God, I will never leave you or forget you.'

'I'd like to meet Rosa. Can you bring her?'

'Sure . . .'

Helen smiled and closed her eyes.

'I was up in New York recently. On business.'

'Did you visit the old neighborhood?'

Nathan nodded.

'Still the same?'

'It's certainly not the shithole we knew.'

'Did you visit daddy's grave?'

'You have to be kidding.'

Helen's eyes closed for a moment. 'Every day is so long, Nathan. They give me my pills, and I watch TV.'

'What's your favorite program right now?'

'*American Idol*. You ever watch that?'

Nathan shook his head.

'It's crazy. There's this English guy, Simon Cowell, who is so mean to everyone. I can't believe he's allowed to say such things about people who are just trying their best.'

'It's the way of the world.'

Helen got that faraway look in her eyes. Then tears began to roll down her cheeks. 'I sometimes think of mummy. I don't blame her for leaving us.'

'Neither do I.'

'You know what I remember about her?'

Nathan shook his head.

'Her wavy hair.'

'What else do you remember about her?'

'She was always crying.'

Half an hour later, Nathan was cruising through the heart of Little Havana, a little slice of old Cuba on Calle Ocho – 8th Street – between 12th and 27nd Avenues. All the signs were in Spanish. He wound down his window and a caught a strong whiff of shrimp wafting from a big seafood restaurant. Old men sat smoking outside neon-lit bars.

He spotted Rosa, sitting demurely outside Domino Park under some palms, and pulled up to the kerb. She pecked him on the cheek as she climbed in beside him. She smelled of expensive perfume.

'Thought you were going to stand me up,' she said.

'Why would I do anything so stupid?'

'I know what you Americans are like. You have a little fun, then you don't wanna know.'

Nathan smiled, feeling crazier than he had for days.

'So, where you taking me?'

'It's a surprise.'

'I like surprises.'

Nathan took the South Dixie Highway, switched on some Georgia Satellites and relaxed to the rocking blues riffs. He stole a glance at Rosa who was smiling broadly and running her hand through her wavy black hair.

They headed past affluent Kendall, then the Palmetto golf course, on into the south Florida night.

'Nathan, you mind telling me where we're going?'

'How does an exclusive restaurant, the other side of Florida City, sound?'

'Great. As long as you're paying.'

Florida City laid claim to be the southernmost city in America which was not an island. They drove past seedy hotels, motels and diners. Soon the last remnants of civilization had disappeared in his rear-view mirror. Ten minutes later Nathan turned along a dirt road and pulled up in a glade of pines, headlights on, engine still running.

'What are we stopping here for, Nathan? You run out of gas?'

'Wait there a second.'

He got out of the car, walked to the back and opened the trunk. Inside, the plastic sheeting was in place, along with the rope and some duct tape.

45

The investigation was back to square one after the explanation from Cunningham's deputy. It completely threw Deborah. But two days later Robert Sommers made contact, saying he wanted to help.

He got a note to Deborah as before, in her mailbox, asking her to meet up that night at Delano's Blue Door restaurant in the heart of South Beach.

Deborah didn't think it made sense. Surely, the scandal and the embarrassing pictures emblazoned across the *Enquirer* and the Internet would have sent most men scurrying for cover.

So why not Sommers?

The restaurant was located on Collins Avenue, a fashionable hang-out. It was decadence writ large: white candles, billowing floor-to-ceiling white drapes, high ceilings and a stunning white grand piano. Not surprisingly, it was a magnet for those who wanted to be seen, including movie and pop stars, not to mention a sprinkling of supermodels and trust-fund kids, showing off.

Deborah and Jamille joined Sommers on the outdoor verandah overlooking a peaceful garden, which bizarrely included a life-size chessboard.

After they'd ordered drinks, Sommers, wearing a beige linen suit and pale blue novelty tie, asked for the latest on Deborah's investigation. He listened intently as she gave him an update following the conversation with Cunningham's number two.

'Leave aside what happened to me for just a moment, if that's possible,' he said. 'I've got my own thoughts on that. But all this talk of a mole within the ranks at Langley sounds like the paranoid ravings emanating from Langley during the Cold War. Puts me in mind of James Angleton. You remember him?'

Deborah nodded. 'CIA's counter-intelligence chief in the 1960s and 1970s, right?'

'Certifiable, by all accounts,' Sommers said. 'He was also an obsessive when it came to internal spy-hunts. He saw Communists everywhere.' Sommers sipped his glass of Napa Valley Cabernet Sauvignon and smiled, looking at Deborah. 'At Langley the joke used to do the rounds that Angleton ended up believing he was a goddamn spy as well. He was there for thirty years in this crazy delusional state. And that paranoia spread and became endemic within the agency.'

Deborah nodded. 'So are you suggesting that now we're talking about disinformation rather than paranoia?'

Sommers smiled. 'What do you think?'

'A classic case. The object being to confuse and mislead, to conceal what has really happened.'

'I can quite see why your publisher got cold feet,' Sommers said. 'But I don't understand why Cunningham palmed you off with his number two.'

He went quiet as a handsome young Latino waiter came over to take their orders. Deborah chose crab cake and Maine lobster. Sommers chose pan-seared lamb chops and Jamille plumped for fillet of sea bass.

Before resuming the conversation Sommers waited until the young man politely collected the menus. 'The question is where do you go from here, Deborah?'

'Well,' she said, putting down her glass of Perrier, 'I checked up on Cunningham and I noticed that he used to be the CIA's top guy in Guatemala, in the 1980s. The agency was lurking in the shadows as murders, abductions and disappearances of any dissenters were carried out by those in power. No one seriously doubts that the CIA was turning a blind eye to a regime they were backing. There were also allegations that they secretly boosted aid to the military. Cunningham might be a breath of fresh air, but he has skeletons in his closet. And it doesn't require a great stretch of the imagination to realize that the CIA was responsible for the deaths of John Hudson and Richard Turner, does it?'

'Let's get back to some facts,' Sommers said. 'The documents you have are crucial to this whole thing. I don't believe for one second they are fakes. But if you are going to make this stick, Deborah, the best plan of action is perseverance. You've given them something to think about, and I suggest you leave this ball in Michael Cunningham's court and let him stew.'

'What about authentication?' Deborah asked.

Sommers drained his glass of red wine and smiled. 'One step at a time, Deborah. Let them make the next move.'

Just after one a.m., as Deborah awoke from a doze to find the television still on, CNN were showing the latest outrage in Iraq – a multiple suicide bombing in Baghdad despite the massive 'surge' in the city by US troops.

Her cellphone rang. It was Robert Sommers. 'Can we talk?'

Deborah switched off the TV with the remote, not wishing to wake Jamille who was sleeping in the spare room. 'Do you know what time it is, Robert?'

'I can't sleep, like you. Listen to this. I just received a very interesting call from a friend of mine who knows Cunningham. He says that everything that has happened can be traced back to this one guy who is known to those within Langley. I asked him to be a bit more precise. Apparently this guy was part of the NCS.'

Deborah knew that meant National Clandestine Service. Sommers had explained that before. 'Not good, right?'

'This guy has been all over. He's worked psychological ops in Central America, Iraq, Eastern Europe. He's a real hard case.'

'So where is he now?' Deborah asked, knowing the answer.

'Right here. In Florida.'

'And they reckon this is the same guy who killed John Hudson?'

'Yes. Deborah . . . I believe he is following orders from those at the very top.'

Deborah said nothing.

'Question is, is this more disinformation to put you off the scent, to stop you going after Cunningham? To put the frighteners on. I think you need to take great care.'

Deborah shivered. 'I'm starting to feel like a fly in a spider's web.'

'I think you should get out of your condo. You're a sitting target. Look what happened to me. That was a cute set-up. Trust me – they'll stop at nothing.'

46

Less than an hour later Deborah had packed a bag, picked up some essentials including the documents and her laptop, and was being driven through the near-deserted dark streets to the relative safety of Jamille's small house in affluent suburban Pinecrest, a hundred yards from Gulliver Preparatory School.

She managed to grab a couple of hours' sleep on the couch before being woken just after dawn, when Jamille's kids piled into the living room and switched on the TV. The news showed footage of the Hyatt and the compromising photos of Sommers. In a strange place, with Sam still in hospital, Deborah felt that her whole life had become surreal.

After showering and changing, she and Jamille went along to Hudson's funeral at Woodlawn Park Cemetery in Little Havana, amid the splendor of Gothic statues, granite angels, and marble crypts. Hundreds of mourners attended. Scores of them were in their late teens and early twenties, some dressed casually, probably college friends of John.

As the coffin was lowered into the rock-hard earth, Bill Hudson, dressed in an immaculate dark suit, black tie and white shirt, wept openly, and his wife Kate fell to her knees.

The sky was the most perfect blue, but the sound of a mother's helpless grief in the still, humid air sounded like the wail of a wounded animal.

Faith called Deborah later that afternoon.

'I don't want any excuses, girl,' she said. 'I mean it.'

Deborah laughed. 'I'll be there, don't worry.'

'You better, otherwise I'll be dropping you for the next game.'

'I'll be there, Faith, I promise.'

'You hear Gloria's news?'

'I thought she wasn't due for another fortnight?'

'Twins. Can you believe it? Goddamn – Gloria a mother? Listen, the girls are heading across to the South Miami Hospital tomorrow night. You wanna tag along?'

'I'll try.'

'Good. Anyway, I wanna see you shakin' what you've got tonight. You hear me?'

Deborah laughed. 'You just watch me.'

She hung up and leaned back in her seat, thinking about Gloria Tillett. She had fought her way out of Overtown, like most of the girls. Previously she'd worked the streets, feeding her crack habit, but after leaving her abusive pimp husband she had put herself through school with some of the money she'd saved and become a successful businesswoman, organizing conferences across south Florida. The previous year she'd got married again, to a funny, kind man called George Manders, who owned a couple of garages in Coconut Grove where they now lived happily together.

Increasingly, Deborah found herself wondering what it would be like to have children. She knew that Sam would be a good father. But she was not at all sure how she would handle things.

She checked her e-mails on her BlackBerry. But there was nothing important. She then began surfing the Net on Jamille's laptop, killing some time before she headed down to Palmer Park.

Trawling through the *New York Daily News* website she spotted Pam Molloy's byline emblazoned on the front page. She had an exclusive on a young boy being gunned down by police raiding a crack den in the Bronx. Having children was a big responsibility. And could bring great pain.

Deborah clicked on to the paper's archive and pulled up a few articles on the CIA director, Michael Cunningham, in which dire predictions of a 'twenty-year onslaught' against Islamic terrorists were made. There was another short piece about a private function in New York at The Waldorf that had been hosted by the Saudi Consulate General.

Her gaze lingered on the black and white photograph taken one month earlier. On the far left of the picture was a man in a formal dinner suit. The Deputy Head of the CIA. His name was Charles Henke.

'You okay?' Jamille asked from the doorway.

'I'm fine. Just thinking about what Robert was saying last night, about disinformation and about the way the CIA works. What if we're only scraping the surface? What if this whole thing goes deeper within Langley? Maybe a network. A cabal working to their own agenda.'

'Girl, you really are crazy.'

'Then I got to thinking about Cunningham. I have been focusing almost exclusively on speaking to him. But what do we know about Cunningham's number two?'

Jamille crouched down beside the screen. 'Is that him?'

'Yup. He's tipped to take over at the end of the year. He's the man I spoke to. The man who spun me the line about a spy within.'

'So?'

'Now I'm thinking it might be a very good idea to know more about him . . .'

Just over an hour later Deborah was sweating profusely under the floodlights at Palmer Park, doing killer relay sprints up and down the pitch.

'Call that effort?' Faith barked from the sidelines. 'Don't think you're fooling me, girls. Dig deeper. Come on, let's see you! You think I do this for the good of my health?'

Deborah gritted her teeth, feeling her calf muscles tighten minute by minute.

'We might not be the most talented team in the league, but we sure as hell are the fittest.'

Deborah's heart was pounding as the sprints continued.

'This is for your benefit. You want the girls from Hialeah to beat us down in the last few minutes? Ain't nobody stronger than us. And ain't nobody gonna come close to us this season. Pain? You call this pain? Just suck it up. And you will get stronger, fitter and meaner. You hearin' me, girls?'

The rest of the session was taken up by passing and moving, dribbling and shooting. Afterwards, mentally and physically spent, Deborah threw her sports bag into the trunk of her car.

'You gave it your all tonight, honey.' Faith came over and patted her on the back. 'Show the same commitment at the weekend and we'll go top of the league.'

'I'll do my best.'

On the side of the pitch a Lexus pulled up and two thickset men in smart suits stepped out.

'What the hell is going on here?' Jamille said as they both flashed their Miami-Dade police badges.

'Miss Deborah Jones?' the older of the two asked. 'Do you know a Robert Sommers?'

'Yes, I do. Sorry, is there a problem?' Deborah said.

The detective's face remained impassive. 'Miss Jones,

I'm sorry to say that we're going to have to bring you in for questioning.'

'Hang on just a minute . . . What is it?'

'We'd rather you accompanied us down to HQ.'

'If you've got some questions I'll answer them in front of my friends, if you don't mind.'

'Very well. Did Mr Sommers call you around one o'clock this morning?'

'Yes, he did.'

'What did you discuss?'

'An investigation I was working on. I can't say any more. Why?'

'Miss Jones, we believe you were the last person he called from his cellphone.'

'Last person? How?'

'Robert Sommers is dead. He was found by a maid just over an hour ago in his bathtub at the Hyatt.'

47

The clouds were swollen with rain when Harry Donovan's flight touched down at Miami. He yawned as he headed home across the causeway for a quick shower and change of suit. He hadn't slept a wink since his conversation with Jackie. Turning along South Mashta Drive, he saw the huge palms lining the street bending in the wind. He felt knots of tension in his stomach at the prospect of seeing his wife again.

As he glided through the electronic gates and into the driveway of his home he wondered what kind of mood she would be in.

'Hey, honey, only me,' he shouted, as he shut the front door.

Harry dumped his briefcase and bags, wondering where his wife was. He checked in the kitchen, then upstairs in the bedroom. He heard the shower in the bathroom. Then he went through to his study.

He shut the door behind him and switched on his laptop to check his e-mails. Quite a lot from Juan. He reached over the filing cabinet beside his desk and pulled out the bottom drawer. He flicked through several folders but couldn't find the budget cuts that Juan was proposing.

Strange. He remembered going over the figures the previous day before he'd left for the airport. He was sure he'd put the file away.

'Honey,' he said again as he headed into the bathroom.

Jackie shrieked when he opened the door. She was wrapped in a huge fluffy towel and was drying her hair. 'Shit, don't ever do that,' she snapped.

'Sorry.' He pecked her on the cheek. 'Honey, did you tidy up some of my files by any chance?'

'Me? Why on earth would I do that?'

'I don't know . . . By mistake?'

Jackie stopped drying her hair and scowled at him. 'Harry, you know damn well that I never touch anything in your study. Only Concheeta.'

'Where is she?'

'She's off today and tomorrow. Vacation. Even servants are entitled to a short break, Harry. But she knows it's more than her job's worth to touch any of your stuff.'

'I need to go over those figures before I see Juan,' Harry said.

'Don't look at me.'

228

Harry turned on his heel and stormed downstairs, muttering under his breath. He fixed himself a coffee, wondering if he hadn't indeed misplaced the file. But after racking his brain he felt sure that the papers had been put straight back in the filing cabinet.

He went through to the living room and switched on Fox & Friends. John McCain was grinning beside Cindy, his glamorous wife and former opiate-addict, who was running her hand through her platinum-blonde hair and wearing an expensive lilac suit and pearls. Her smile was rigid. Facelifts were great, Harry reflected, if you just wanted the one expression.

It was common knowledge that the business and political contacts of Cindy McCain's father had helped John McCain to gain a foothold in Arizona politics, just as Jackie and her family's extensive contacts had been instrumental in the behind-the-scenes lobbying to help Harry secure the executive editorship of the *Miami Herald*. Harry's political beliefs, not too different from McCain's, had brought him to the attention of those who wielded power, including Michael Cunningham who had long-standing links to the paper, one of the biggest opinion formers in Florida. Big military, low taxes, vehemently anti-Castro – Harry knew he ticked all the boxes, unlike Sam Goldberg who was considered a 'bit of a crazy' by Cunningham.

'You find what you were searching for?' Jackie came into the living room, resplendent in a sleek pale yellow suit.

'I'll have a look later.' Harry switched off the TV with the remote.

They went through to the kitchen together. 'Good trip?'

'Had better.'

'You eaten?'

Harry picked up the copy of that day's *Herald* and studied the front page. Iraq, city corruption charges and the suicide of a nightclub boss. 'I'm fine. Thanks.'

As his wife put on a fresh pot of coffee and made some toast, he suddenly realized how quiet it was.

'Where's Roxy?' he said, referring to the family Doberman which was usually around.

'I don't know – I just got up. I assumed he was down here.'

'So where the hell is he?'

Harry's cellphone rang, abruptly interrupting the conversation.

'I have some interesting news for you.' It was the educated voice again.

Harry indicated to his wife that he was heading upstairs to take the call and she nodded back at him.

'I'm tired of these games,' he said, slightly out of breath as he slumped in his leather study chair, shutting the door behind him. 'I want you out of my life.'

'All in good time. We just wanted to make sure that you hadn't forgotten our little talk.'

'You said you had some news for me.'

'I believe Sam Goldberg is going to be released from

hospital tomorrow. You know what that means? He's going to want this investigation to proceed. And he's going to wonder why his attractive investigations editor isn't allowed on the premises.'

'I'll deal with it.'

'I don't think you understand.'

'What don't I understand?'

'I'm not convinced you've got the message. About just how serious we are. Do you want me to tell you what we found in the middle of the night?'

'Found?'

'In your home. While you were gone.'

Harry sat bolt upright.

'Relax. We just wanted to show you how easy it would be to get to you. Or to your wife. Or anyone dear to you, if this proceeds.'

Harry dreaded what he was going to hear next.

'I'm just reading these projections for 2009/10 at the *Herald*. Very ambitious plans. If this was leaked to the *Sentinel*, I don't know—'

'This is stopping. And it's stopping right now.'

'This is the last time I will ever call you. I just wanted you to be aware that any attempt to resurrect this investigation, or to contact the police or even the feds, will not be tolerated.'

Harry took some deep breaths to calm himself down. Then he went downstairs and relayed the conversation to his wife who was staring fixedly out of the window.

She didn't look round.

'What is it?' he asked.

Suddenly, Jacqueline put her hand to her mouth and started screaming.

Down below, floating on its side in the pool, was their dog, blood trailing from its neck.

48

The gurney bearing the black body bag that contained the bloodstained body of Robert Sommers was wheeled out of a side entrance of the Hyatt by uniformed cops. Parked diagonally across the street was Nathan Stone, his shades on and New York Mets hat pulled down low. He pretended to read his paper but couldn't keep his eyes off the van with the blacked-out windows.

As the van pulled away he followed at a safe distance.

Nathan lit a cigarette as he tailed the morgue van. From Coral Gables it wound its way in bumper-to-bumper traffic along the South Dixie Highway to the downtown towers. He pulled up close by the three-building complex which comprised the state-of-the-art Joseph H. Davis Center for Forensic Pathology, which was located at the edge of the sprawling Jackson

Memorial Hospital and the University of Miami Medical School campus.

Nathan's cellphone rang.

'The networks are calling it suicide,' the familiar voice said. 'You done good.'

'What else are they saying?'

'Exactly what we wanted them to say. Robert Sommers killed himself after being caught with a Cuban call girl. Tragic.'

Nathan took one last drag of his cigarette and dropped the end out of the window.

'Did he say anything before he died?'

'Like what?'

'Like how many copies of the fucking documents are still kicking around?'

'Said he had seen a hard copy Deborah had but didn't have a clue where it was being kept. He took a long time just to tell me that.'

'Shit, Nathan. How did you allow him to get so close?'

'He fooled me. I didn't have a clue which train he was going to take until it was too late.'

'We've got a decision pending. And it's going to be made in the next twelve hours.'

'Sam Goldberg is the key. If we keep him in our sights, then we'll have her.'

'Is it getting too much for you, Nathan? You want a vacation?'

'Not now. I'm starting to enjoy myself. Just like the old days.'

'It is important that you stay completely focused.'

'Once this business is over I'll take off for a couple of months. But until then I'm your man.'

Nathan stared across the street as a large car pulled up outside the morgue bureau. Out stepped a good-looking gentleman in a well-cut dark suit. Nathan allowed himself a wry smile.

Dr Brent Simmons was carrying a briefcase.

49

Sam was dressed and ready for Doborah. He was sitting in an easy chair beside his bed. His face looked pinched and his clothes were hanging off him. Sam's sisters hugged Deborah tight when she arrived.

'You both need to slow down, honey,' Lauren said. 'You're killing yourself with this investigation.'

'Sam said you fancied Barbados, Deborah,' Miriam added. 'I know a great retreat on the west coast.'

'Maybe once this is all over.' Deborah smiled as she crouched down beside Sam and held his hand before kissing it lightly. 'You made it, tough guy.'

Sam nodded. 'Not so tough. But I got the all-clear. Doctor says I've got to take it easy for a little while.'

To her surprise, Deborah found herself in tears.

Later in the afternoon Deborah and Sam were picked up by Thomas McNally with two of his men in tow.

They headed for McNally's place on Fisher Island. Deborah strapped herself into the back seat of the SUV – Sam was in the front – as they drove at high speed, with several counter-surveillance U-turns along the way, until they got to the ferry terminal beside the Macarthur Causeway. From there it was only a seven-minute journey across to the exclusive island home of the super-rich. A huge cruise ship was just docking at the port.

Deborah turned to McNally as they reached the gate-house. 'Are you sure this is okay with your wife?'

'Andrea? Are you crazy? She's already got your rooms made up – they overlook the water. New laptop for you, Deborah, and for Sam, so you don't have to head into the office. You should have let me know earlier.'

'You're very kind.'

'Happy to help.'

The barrier lifted up and the guard saluted as they drove through. Huge palm trees shrouded the entrance to the white stucco house. A beautiful woman dressed in pale pink was waiting at the top of the gravel drive.

'Call me Andrea,' she said, kissing Deborah on the cheek. Deborah noted the expensive perfume. Then she hugged Sam.

'This is all too much,' he said. 'You shouldn't have.'

'Nonsense, Sam. You're guests, so you've got the run of the whole house. Anything you want, just holler.'

It was cool inside. Terracotta floors, modern art on the whitewashed walls, floor-to-ceiling windows over-looking the moonlit water.

Deborah's room had a waterside view. Gleaming luxury yachts bobbed in the heavy swell. The decor was cool beige throughout and there were starched white cotton sheets on the bed with a large lamp on either side. A new laptop was already switched on.

'You won't be bothered here unless you want to be,' Sam said.

'I need to work. You know that.'

'Can't you just take it easy for once?'

'You know what I'm like.'

Sam smiled and held her close. She could feel how he had lost weight, and there was a fragility to him that made her ache with tenderness.

Andrea fixed them a chicken salad with French fries and a couple of bottles of Diet Coke. Then they all sat outside on the deck.

Deborah held Sam's hand and immediately felt better. McNally fixed himself a large Jack Daniel's and his wife a white wine spritzer. Deborah noticed Sam casting a wistful eye at the whiskey. But, dutifully, he swallowed his Diet Coke.

'Helluva face the guy left you with,' McNally said.

Sam laughed. 'You don't think it makes me look more rugged?'

'Just makes you look more of any ugly bastard than you were in the first place.'

They sat for a while in a companionable silence. The air smelled sweet.

'Deborah, I believe you or Sam or both of you were

probably being followed,' McNally said eventually, 'and it is possible that part of the problem was your cell-phones.'

'You mean my phone was bugged? Or Sam's?'

McNally smiled. 'All cellphones have microphones and advanced technology fitted as standard. It is perfectly easy for government agencies, and I'm talking primarily the NSA and FBI, to monitor what you're saying, if your cellphone is on your desk or in your pocket, wherever. It's a roving bug. And it's not even illegal. There was a case at the end of last year where it was revealed that the feds were listening in to some of the most powerful guys in the Genovese family via their cellphones. The judge ruled that it was legal because federal wiretapping law allows the authorities to listen in on conversations that take place near a suspect's cellphone.'

'So the CIA could listen in on my conversations if my cellphone was just lying around on my kitchen table, or on a restaurant table, or in my back pocket? Even if it was switched off?' Deborah was surprised that neither Sam nor she knew about this.

'Kinda scary, huh? The only way to beat it is to remove the cellphone battery.'

'So how is this done?' Sam asked.

'What usually happens is that software is remotely installed on a handset without you, me or anyone knowing anything about it. The microphone is then acti-vated, even if the goddamn thing is turned off. You could be in a meeting with Deborah, both your phones switched off, but people could be listening in. I have some of the best counter-surveillance experts in the world on my payroll and they have worked for government agencies. The American government is the world leader in this field and I can say, without a word of a lie, that their intelligence agencies use this technique on a daily basis.'

'That's unbelievable,' Deborah said.

'Think about it. A cellphone sitting on the desk of a newspaper editor, reporter, or politician can be transformed into a powerful bug, enabling certain agencies to listen in. And no one will be any the wiser.'

Deborah said, 'Everyone has a cellphone these days, even my mother.'

'That's why I've taken the liberty of removing the batteries from your old phones, in effect disabling them, and have supplied both you and Sam with two new cellphones for the duration of this investigation so that you can't be monitored. They're activated, and they're waiting in your bedrooms for you to use immediately. I got them from Israel.'

Deborah leaned over and patted McNally on the back of his hand. 'I appreciate all you're doing for us, Mr McNally. Really I do. And I'm impressed.'

'God, it's good to be out of hospital,' Sam said. 'And how wonderful to have such friends.'

50

The women went to bed early but Sam was savoring his escape from intensive care and was glad to stay up a little longer, even without the aid of a couple of shots of Jack Daniel's.

'Hey, before I forget, I've got something for you,' McNally said. He got up and went inside, returning a few moments later with a buff file.

'Deborah asked for this,' he said. 'All she needs to know about Charles Woodrow Henke. And I mean *everything*. Makes interesting reading.'

'Can I take a look?'

McNally shrugged and handed it over. 'You're paying for it, man.'

Sam scanned the pages quickly. 'Well, well, well,' he said. 'So his wife loses a fortune regularly on the blackjack tables in Vegas.'

'Nobody's perfect.'

'Says here that Henke started off his military life in the marines. Served in Beirut and Afghanistan in the 1980s with the CIA. Served as an "adviser" to the Colombian government and the Contra rebels. Maybe Deborah really is on to something. In the 1990s he was helping the Iraqis in the war against Iran. Reassigned to the Armed Forces Institute of Pathology for six months.' Sam saw the connection immediately: Simmons and Henke. But he didn't let on. 'Station chief in Beirut and then in Kabul. Also worked in Riyadh. Nice crowd he hangs out with.'

'Read on. It gets even more interesting.'

'He left the military for a five-year stint as the chief operating officer of Platinum Security Solutions. Never heard of them.'

'Very low-profile. They supply thousands of security personnel, advisers and bodyguards – ex-Special Forces and the like – to Iraq, Afghanistan and other trouble spots.'

Sam scanned a two-page Wall Street report. 'Business is booming, share price at an all-time high. Good time to own Platinum stock.'

'Read on, man.'

'"A 1.2 billion-dollar five-year contract with the Saudi oil ministry has transformed the fortunes of this previously moribund company since Henke took over the reins,"' Sam quoted from the report.

'Apparently Charles Henke has contacts on Capitol Hill, in the Pentagon and at the highest levels of this administration. He has a lot of muscle. And he's biding his time to become director, which could be within the next three months. But that's not all. I gather his ties to the Saudis are cause for concern within the Agency.'

'How come?'

'He's a regular at the Saudi Embassy. I even heard a rumor that he has a townhouse in Georgetown which was paid for by the Saudis. I'm also told, by one of my best sources, that Henke has taken over at Langley. He calls the shots. The official line is that Cunningham has been based for the last few months in Baghdad, with occasional trips across to Kabul. But I'm hearing serious whispers that that is not the case.'

'Are you saying that Cunningham isn't in Iraq?'

'Shortly after Charles Henke joined, and I'm talking a matter of weeks, Cunningham had some sort of breakdown. No one knows why. But the White House was terrified that this would leak out. He is recuperating at a military facility in California.'

'Jesus. Sounds like a fucking *coup d'état*.'

'Sam, want a bit of advice?'

'Shoot.'

'I would never dream of telling you whether to continue with an investigation or not. That's your business. But these guys are dangerous. You were lucky. Sommers wasn't.'

'You don't believe that shit about a mole inside the CIA?'

'It's not out of the question. Remember Aldrich Ames?'

Sam nodded, recalling the case of the former CIA counter-intelligence officer and analyst – and alcoholic – who had been passing secrets to the Soviets for years. 'You reckon Henke could have gone bad?'

'I think you need to shake the tree. Call him. Tell him you don't believe the line he's pushing. Say you're going to pass what you've got to the Senate Select Committee on Intelligence. Nobody fucks with them.'

'What if he says fine, go right ahead?'

'Hand over the documents to the chairman, Harold Steinberg. He'll find out if they are fakes or not. And it also keeps you in the clear, in case Henke's story really should stack up.'

Sam considered the idea for a few moments. The Senator was a wily old-style Democrat and wasn't afraid to confront the powers-that-be. 'I don't know. We need something more concrete. Further proof. But my priority just now is Deborah. How can I keep her safe?'

Sam stayed on the deck alone after McNally turned in. He was startled by a sound. The French doors opened. It was Deborah. She was wearing a large oversize white shirt and was barefoot.

'You okay?' he asked.

She smiled. 'Couldn't sleep. I heard Thomas clomping around upstairs, so I decided to join you, if that's okay. It's nice here.'

Deborah sat down beside Sam and he reached out for her hand, squeezing it tight. The moonlight cast a pale light on her honey-brown skin. Deborah stared out over the water, soaking up the tranquility, breathing in the balmy south Florida night air, feeling at peace. They sat in a dreamy silence for what seemed like an eternity, watching ibises swooping down low on the still waters of the Cut.

'Don't let me be alone tonight, Sam,' Deborah said. 'I don't ever want to be alone again. I've never been so scared as I've been these last few days.'

Sam felt his throat tighten. For a few seconds he just smiled at her, admiring her beauty, glad that she was by his side. Then he leaned over and kissed her lightly on the cheek. He smelled the sweetest perfume.

'I want you to be with me tonight, Sam. I want you to be with me every night.'

They stood up and she put her arms around his neck and pulled him close. 'I need you, Sam.'

He kissed her long and hard. Then, arms around each other's waists, they went inside.

51

The beam of white light from the Cape Florida Lighthouse – on the southernmost point of Key Biscayne – strafed the dark, oppressive Miami sky every five seconds as shards of blood-red sky appeared on the horizon. Harry Donovan breathed hard as he pounded the beach on an early-morning jog, unable to sleep, not knowing what to do or who to talk to. Sweat poured down his face.

Why the hell did they have to kill the dog? Even with Sam due back, the investigation didn't have a chance in hell of making it into the paper with both him and Juan united in their resolve.

His cellphone rang and he interrupted his run to answer.

'Hey, honey,' his wife said, 'Where are you? I just woke up and you were gone.'

'Trying to stretch my legs, that's all,' he panted. 'I need time to think.'

'Honey, don't shut me out. I understand how you must feel under pressure, Harry. But so do I.'

Using the back of his hand, Harry wiped the sweat from his brow.

'Go and speak to Ron. I know that's the right thing to do. The feds will understand,' Jacqueline said.

'Jackie, we need to think long and hard about this. There are implications for everyone.'

'You're being really so indecisive.'

'If I go to the feds today, there's no turning back.'

'You mean the fallout if that conversation with Cunningham was recorded?'

'I'm way past caring about that shit.'

'It'll be fine, Harry.'

'You didn't wake up while someone was in our house and killed the goddamn dog. They didn't leave a trace. Nothing on camera, even. If I'm going to speak to the feds, I want to be absolutely sure that my wife, my son and my son's mother, are safe. You've got to trust me on this.'

'For how long?'

'Forty-eight hours, max.'

'Promise?'

'I promise.'

He ended the call. Almost immediately his cellphone rang again. 'Donovan,' he sighed.

'Harry, Eddie Rafferty here.' It was the *Herald*'s abrasive ex-publisher who had retired six months earlier.

'Eddie, how the hell are you?'

'We need to talk.'

'You wanna meet up for lunch?'

'No. I want to see you in the newsroom asap.'

Eddie Rafferty was in Juan's plush corner office. He had put on even more weight and was bursting out of his dark blue pin-striped suit. He stood up slowly and shook Harry's hand.

'Nice to see you again,' he said, slumping back down in his seat.

Harry Donovan pulled up a chair opposite Rafferty. 'I thought you had retired to Key Largo?'

'Not any more,' Rafferty replied. 'I'm the paper's new publisher.'

'Sorry, am I missing something here?'

'I've been brought in to sort out this mess.'

'What the hell are you talking about?'

'I'm talking about the breakdown in trust between the *Miami Herald*'s managing editor, Sam Goldberg, and the publisher, Juan Garcia. Is that right?'

'This is outrageous! Why haven't I been notified?'

'You have. The letter from Steve Ronin is on your desk. Why don't you go check it out?'

Harry shifted in his seat. 'I will.'

'Steve is the chairman of the company which owns the *Herald*, but—'

'I know who Steve Ronin is.'

'Someone is trying to silence this paper. A clear

248

warning was sent to Sam and Deborah that the investigation was to be halted.'

'How the hell did you get involved?'

'Sam contacted Steve yesterday from the hospital, and he got the whole low-down. Steve didn't even know he was in hospital. That's outrageous.'

Harry said nothing.

'So he contacted me to see if I could help out over the next six months, until the situation is resolved.'

'Is that right?'

'Look, I'm not casting aspersions on you. Let's be quite clear about that.'

'Then what the hell *are* you doing, goddamit?'

'Getting the *Miami Herald* back to doing what it does best. And by that I mean not shrinking from difficult stories and crumbling at the first hint of pressure.'

'You think that's what I did?'

'I think that's what Juan did. He made a wrong call. You were merely loyal.' Rafferty shifted in his seat. 'It's your job, Harry, to resist pressure from any intelligence agency or any arm of government. Do you understand?'

Harry's mind was whirling.

'This is Juan's first major position with a major American newspaper and I believe that his experience as a publisher, albeit a highly successful one, wasn't best suited to this particular role. As you know, Harry, Juan's father is a prominent figure in the Cuban-American community here in Miami and swears unswerving allegiance to the Stars and Stripes. Frankly, I think that Juan was suckered.'

'Obviously I'm going to have to consider my position.'

'You read the documents Deborah unearthed, didn't you?'

'Yes, I did. But there was an authentication question.'

'Run it by the CIA. That's what Deborah's been trying to do.' Rafferty leaned forward, hands clasped together on the desk. 'Let me be quite clear. The investigation is now back on. Sam needs a few more days to recuperate. Meanwhile, Deborah can get things back on track . . . Look, if you're not happy . . .' Rafferty paused. 'Sam wants you to stay put. He thinks you're a solid executive editor, and he admires the job you do.'

Harry could not conceal the truth any longer. It all came tumbling out. The calls at the country club. The photos to the house. The dead dog. The blackmail.

'Jesus Christ, Harry.' Rafferty leaned back in his seat. 'Why didn't you say? This changes everything. Have you called in the police?'

'I don't know if I trust the cops not to leak this whole goddamn affair all over the networks. I have to make sure my family is safe.'

'Absolutely.'

'After that, I want to speak to the feds direct. I know their top man in Miami.'

'So do I. He's a good guy.'

Harry nodded.

'Let's get the morning meeting out of the way and then sort things out. How does that sound?'

'You want to fire my ass, don't you?'

'Harry, you're a good guy doing a tough job. I've made a ton of mistakes in my time. The trick is to learn from them.'

52

Nathan Stone sat in his car in the *Herald* employee parking lot as a train thundered by on the Metro track above. He was listening to a playback of the conversation again. He closed his eyes tight to block out the noise of the train. He could hear the strain in their voices. A short while later, his phone rang.

'Okay, here's what's going to happen, Nathan,' the familiar voice said. 'He is about to sing. He's also one of a handful who've seen the documents. His wife has just left the house.'

'So it's only him I have to worry about?'

'Precisely. I don't think he'll go home until this afternoon at the earliest. Which gives you time. But I'll keep you posted.'

'What's my best line of approach, bearing in mind my previous visit?'

'Take the boat right up to their jetty, just like the last time.'

'What's the cover story?'

'Property developer wanting to buy their house.'

'Security system?'

'It's been deactivated remotely.'

Nathan pulled a packet of cigarettes out of his top pocket. Then he lit up, exhaling slowly, as he pressed the windows down. 'How's DC?'

'Full of assholes. But you know that already.'

'You can say that again.'

'I've managed to pull a few strings to get your sister a nice room at the new facility. You don't have to worry about that.'

'We've only got each other, man. Not a fucking soul cares about us.'

'Nathan, *I* care about her. She will be looked after. And so will you. Come what may.'

'Tell me about the electrics.'

'Four years old, gas generator in the basement as back-up.'

'Plumbing?'

'Ten years old.'

A uniformed security guard came into view. Nathan started up his car. 'Where's the boat?'

'Sunset Harbour. Any questions?'

'What's the rate?'

'Quadruple rate. It's been sanctioned.'

'Someone must want this guy out of the way real bad.'

'Oh yeah. Real fucking bad.'

53

Deborah was still sleeping. She looked peaceful, her beautiful black hair contrasting with the starched white pillow on which it rested. Sam stroked her hair and listened to her soft breathing.

For the first time in years he felt at peace. The traumas that he and Deborah had endured during the Hudson investigation could have torn them apart. But the opposite had happened. Their love had grown deeper. Both had broken through their personal problems. They could face the future together with confidence instead of being haunted by their pasts. The threats from the masked intruder had only made them stronger.

Sam got up and swam forty lengths of the infinity pool, his left eye still stinging with the chlorine in the water. Thankfully, the swelling had gone down. And the headaches were gone. It was the most serious exercise he'd done in years. Up and down he swam, as the first pink tinges of dawn touched the dark horizon.

Afterwards, he showered in his plush en-suite bathroom, put on clean clothes – smart suit, shirt – which McNally had got one of his men to pick up along with Deborah's things.

She was still asleep. Sam decided to let her be.

Just after seven, Sam took breakfast with McNally and his wife on the deck, overlooking the choppy blue waters of the Cut. Scrambled egg, rye toast, strong coffee and freshly squeezed orange juice set him up for the day.

'Spoke to the cops over an hour ago,' McNally said, 'and I hear that forensics can't trace the blood left in Deborah's condo. Not a trace.'

'So this guy has no previous – is that what you're saying?'

'Highly unlikely.'

'So what, then?'

'The guy's a ghost, used by the military to do their dirty work.'

'A ghost?'

'That's right. Never leave a trace, because they don't even exist.'

54

Just after midday Deborah awoke. She felt slightly dazed. She and Sam had finally consummated their relationship. After all these years. It took her a few moments to get her bearings in the strange bed as memories of the early hours flooded back. She stared at the white ceiling, fan whirring gently, as a soft buttercup light filtered through the partly open drapes. Then she took a deep breath and smiled.

She got up and went into her bathroom, keen to see how she had changed. Her dark brown eyes were sparkling. She had feared physical intimacy for so long it was like a mental block. But now, for the first time in a long time, she realized she'd slept soundly without waking in a cold sweat. Just the comfort of lying skin-to-skin with the man she loved, falling asleep in his arms. She liked how she looked in the mirror.

After a long hot shower she put on a white T-shirt,

faded jeans and her favorite sneakers. Then she tied her hair back and wandered out onto the deck.

Sam was reading that day's *Herald*. He looked up and smiled. 'Hey, there she is. The Sleeping Beauty.' He stood up and gave her a big hug.

'Now, what can I get you to drink?' Andrea appeared as if by magic. 'Some iced tea, coffee?'

'Iced tea would be great.'

'Something to eat?'

'Any chance of a croissant with strawberry jam – is that all right? It's my favorite.'

'Coming right up.'

'So,' Deborah said, 'have there been any developments while I've been catching up with my beauty sleep?' She sat down in a chair next to Sam and kicked off her shoes.

Sam handed her the file on Henke. She scanned the pages quickly, absorbing the information like a sponge.

'He's our guy,' she said. 'He's behind this. I knew it.'

'Thomas thinks we should get in his face. Shake the tree, so to speak.'

'Risky strategy,' Deborah said. 'Let's not get ahead of ourselves.'

Sam stroked her feet. It felt good. 'I think it'd be best if we hang around here until this blows over.'

'I don't have a problem with that,' said Deborah. And she didn't.

'I called Harry to give him an update of what happened. Told him we'd taken you to a secret location.'

'Thanks for last night, Sam. It was lovely.'

'This is us from now on. No more hiding and living separately.'

'Let's start looking forward. And let's start thinking about our future together.'

'Sounds perfect,' Sam said and kissed her on the lips. 'How's the head?'

'Like new.' He beamed. 'Even if I still look like shit.'

'So, tell me the latest?'

'Harry called to say he's thinking of you.'

'I appreciate that.'

'To be honest, I think Harry's been really shaken up by what's happened.'

'It hasn't been my favorite time either. Till now.'

'Would you mind coming with me to see Bill Hudson later?'

'It'll have to be after the big game with Hialeah this afternoon.'

'You can't be serious, Deborah. This afternoon? With everything that's going on? Is there no one else to take your place?'

'Sam, if I'm not there in precisely two hours' time, Faith will be kicking my ass all over Palmer Park. Trust me, it's not up for discussion. Besides, Jamille will be with me every step of the way.'

'But—'

'Don't worry about me. What about you? Are you sure you feel up to heading across to see Bill?'

'I'm fine. Really.'

Deborah smiled. 'Then that's settled. I'll play the game, and then head straight back here.'

'Thomas thought it would be best if we stayed put. But he's assigned us a special driver cum bodyguard.'

'He'll have to be pretty tough to keep me away from you.' Giggling, Deborah pushed Sam up against the wall and covered his face with kisses.

The broiling sun made conditions for the crunch top-of-the-table clash with Hialeah particularly tough. Drenched in sweat, neither team held back – fierce tackles were the order of the day. Overtown were set up to frustrate their more skillful opponents, soaking up wave after wave of attack. Running hard and moving the ball quickly out of defense to their two speedy wingers, they suddenly had Hialeah on the back foot, urged on by Faith and scores of loyal fans on the sidelines. But just before half-time Overtown were caught in a classic counter-attack. Hialeah scored from a deflected shot on the edge of the Overtown penalty box, their defense nowhere to be found.

Wild celebrations on the touchline spilled over into a heated exchange between Faith and the backroom staff of Hialeah after the goalscorer – swigging a bottle of water a few moments later – spat it out over Faith's sneakers.

A war of words threatened to turn nasty, but the referee and the two linesmen intervened before things escalated.

After a ferocious half-time team talk from Faith, the

Overtown girls' fitness came to the fore, getting the upper hand as the Hialeah players visibly wilted under the unrelenting sun.

A diagonal pass from Deborah to Jamille resulted in a blatant trip, which led to a penalty. Deborah sent the keeper the wrong way, putting Overtown level with only twenty minutes to go.

Then, in the dying seconds of the game, Deborah laid on a defense-splitting pass for Martha Johnston, Overton's lightning-quick full-back, to hammer home a screaming thirty-yard shot into the right-hand top corner, past the despairing efforts of the Hialeah goalkeeper.

The referee's whistle blew, sparking a mini-invasion from Faith and a dozen or so Overtown fans holding Martha aloft. Deborah's team had clinched the title, with two games to spare. Faith was laughing and crying at the same time, all the months of coaching and bawling and shouting paying off with her first league title.

But as the celebrations died down half a dozen young Hispanic men, some sporting Latin King gang tattoos, gathered around them, smoking reefer, talking loudly. They wore black and gold vests, slightly askew matching baseball caps with a gold crown logo, baggy pants and gold necklaces.

'Walk right past them,' Jamille said as she led Deborah to the changing rooms. 'Don't let them bother you.'

Deborah looked straight ahead, focused on the peeling white paint on the dressing-room door, trying to block out the menacing stares.

'What you girls doing tonight?' one of them said 'You turning tricks?'

'Get lost, asshole,' Faith snapped.

One of the group reached out to touch her breasts. Faith lashed out, which only made the gang laugh.

'Don't be like that, ho.' A few high fives.

'Just keep walking,' Jamille said, ushering the rest of the team forward.

The fattest member of the gang, with pockmarked face and bloodshot eyes, barged forward and reached out to grope Jamille between the legs. 'How does that feel, bitch? That feel good?'

In the blink of an eye, Jamille grabbed his right fist and twisted the boy's arm up his back. Then she kicked his legs away from under him and he collapsed in a heap, like a baby elephant.

The gang burst out laughing at their friend's embarrassment.

'Do that again, fat boy,' Jamille said, 'and I'll break your fucking arm.' She eyeballed the ragtag group of friends. None of them looked so cocky. 'Any of you wannabe gangbangers want some of what he got? Do you?'

A scar-faced youth with a goatee just shook his head as he tossed away the butt of his reefer.

Deborah and the rest of the girls headed to the dressing room as the gang drifted away.

As she was being driven back to the Fisher Island ferry by Jamille, Deborah reflected that the mood of euphoria had been soured, the day spoiled.

'Don't worry about those guys,' Jamille said. 'They're just assholes. Don't let them get to you.'

'Easier said than done.'

Later in the afternoon Sam and Deborah were ushered through the gatehouse of Bill Hudson's home. He was standing at the door waiting for them, eyes sunken and a glass of red wine in his hand.

'Glad you could make it,' Bill said. He gave Sam a big hug. 'You okay, big guy?'

'I need to brush up on my martial arts, that's for sure.' Sam put an arm around Deborah's waist. 'Sorry we weren't able to come sooner.'

Bill reached out and shook Deborah's hand. 'Let's go inside.'

The house was all high ceilings, antique French furniture and panoramic views. The three of them were gathered together in the black granite kitchen. An eerie silence pervaded.

'Where's Kate?' Sam asked.

'Not doing too good. She's taken John's death even harder than I have.'

'Look, maybe it's not such a good idea to visit now.'

'Kate's on heavy medication. And I need someone to speak to. Police don't seem at all interested. Think it's a slam-dunk suicide.'

'All I can say is that we're joining up the dots. Slowly. But I've got nothing concrete to tell you yet, Bill.'

The buzzer on a phone attached to the kitchen wall

rang. 'It's the gatehouse,' Bill said. He picked up the phone. 'Hudson.' The color drained immediately from his face. He covered the mouthpiece. 'It's a guy from the morgue. Delivering a few of John's personal belongings. I couldn't face going down there. So they said they'd drop them off instead.'

'Tell him you'll pick it up at the gate,' Sam said. 'Don't let anyone in.'

Two minutes later, Bill returned with a padded brown envelope under one arm. He placed it on the black granite worktop but didn't open it.

Sam put his arm around Bill's shoulders.

'Mr Hudson, if you want we can leave you alone at this moment,' Deborah said.

'There'll be no need for that. But I appreciate the thought.' Bill opened the seal and pulled out a chunky watch and a set of keys. 'The Rolex I gave him for his eighteenth birthday.' He paused for a moment trying to control his emotions. 'I just want him back, that's all. I want him to be home again.'

Bill wiped his eyes with the back of his hand, then picked up the keys. 'That's for his room on campus and his beloved car, his Mercedes convertible.' He looked at the fob – a miniature black plastic car – attached to his keys. 'That's strange. The Mercedes fob is gone. I've never seen this one before.'

'Seems like an old-style Saab,' Deborah said. 'Do you mind if I take a closer look?'

Bill shrugged and handed her the keys.

Deborah ran her finger along the top of the miniature car and then along the side. 'How very clever of John,' she said, opening the small-scale hood. 'You know what that is?'

'Not a clue,' said Sam.

'It's a USB memory stick. You can store vast amounts of information just by inserting this stick into the side of a computer.'

55

Deborah and Sam followed Bill upstairs to his study overlooking the water. Legal tomes and leather-bound books were stacked neatly on shelves from the floor to the ceiling. Beside the window was a large desk, a laptop switched on.

Bill sat down in a burgundy leather chair. 'Well, here goes,' he said and slid the memory stick into the USB port at the side of his computer.

'Password Protected' flashed up immediately. There were seventeen asterisks. Bill slammed the palm of his hand of his desk. 'Goddamit.'

'Okay, it's a setback, but let's try and work it out. Tell me, Bill, what was John's favorite team?'

'Miami Dolphins. But that won't make up seventeen characters, will it?'

'Well, let's put our brains together and see what we can come up with.'

For the next couple of hours they tried numerous passwords. They used the names of famous people that Bill said John had admired – Martin Luther King, Bob Dylan (using his real name Robert Zimmerman) and Bruce Springsteen – but also people he had hated. These included disgraced arch neo-con Paul Wolfowitz, Joseph McCarthy and Howard Kaloogian (founder of the right-wing party Move America Forward). Cities he'd lived in, cities he'd wanted to visit.

But nothing worked.

Eventually they gave up. And Bill made them something to eat.

McNally called in to make sure that everything was okay, and Sam in turn rang Frank Callaghan, who relayed details about a carjacking in Little Havana, a baby girl found alive in a filthy cot in a run-down apartment in Overtown, her crack-addict mother lying dead on the floor, and a soldier who hailed from Fort Lauderdale who'd been killed by a roadside bomb in Baghdad.

Bad news would always be good news for a news-paper.

Deborah sat quietly eating her chicken sandwich. 'Do you mind if I look through John's bedroom, to see if there's anything there that could be used as a password?'

Bill didn't look too convinced but he led the way upstairs in to his son's old room. On one wall, an American flag. And on the other, a black and white poster of Robert Redford and Dustin Hoffman in *All The President's Men*. Two of the four walls had bookshelves, piled high with hundreds of hardback and paperback books. Noticing some of the titles, it was obvious to Deborah where John Hudson's sentiments lay.

She couldn't help but feel sad. The room was laid out exactly as if John was still at home, as if Bill and his wife wanted to preserve it as it had been – where their son had lived and breathed. They seemed unwilling and probably unable to desecrate the evidence of his existence.

Bill went to get his laptop while Sam flicked through hundreds of CDs and DVDs stacked up beside the single bed. He shouted out band names in the hope that they made up seventeen characters. The Velvet Underground, Jerry Lee Lewis and Captain Beefheart.

Deborah began trawling through the shelves of mostly classic novels. When Bill got back she began suggesting author names and book titles. 'Edgar Allan Poe, Patricia Cornwell, Noam Chomsky, Daphne Du Maurier. What about *Stupid White Men* by Michael Moore or *Washington Square* by Henry James?' She ploughed through every piece of fiction and non-fiction that John Hudson had been interested in.

Time was dragging on, and they had not achieved the breakthrough, ignoring the darkness outside.

'Echo and the Bunnymen.' It was a good try from Sam, but there were eighteen characters.

Deborah's gaze was drawn to one well-thumbed book, spine broken, called *Hack Attacks Encyclopedia: A Complete History of Hacks, Cracks, Phreaks, and Spies over Time.*

She began flipping through it at random until she got to a MIT bookmark on page 832.

'Hang on,' she said, scanning the page. 'Wait a goddamn minute.'

Two words leapt out at her. *Microsloth Windows*. It was a disparaging hackerism for Microsoft Windows.

'Bill, try this,' she said.

Suddenly the screen came alive, dozens of documents downloading in seconds. 'Holy shit, what have we here?' Bill cried.

'You're a genius,' Sam said, as they craned over Bill's shoulder to see what came up first.

Dear Mum and Dad,

I am writing this letter to you from a crummy motel on the edge of the Everglades, fearing for my life. I believe they're closing in on me. And this is my only way of talking to you, knowing I may be dead when you read this.

If something happens to me, I hope the contents stored in my memory stick may survive to bear witness to what I know. Folks, I believe I've stumbled onto a conspiracy. Please don't be mad at me. It involves a cabal within the CIA, working against our country for their personal gain. I believe the man at the center of it is Charles Henke, Deputy Director of the CIA. I discovered these documents through hacking into his smartphone and downloading a Trojan virus in a bar in Washington DC, purely to see if there was anything on the twenty-eight missing pages of the Congressional Report into the 9/11 attacks. You know I felt strongly that we should have had that information. And the virus I had co-created cleaned out everything on the guy's phone, which included the unexpurgated version of the 9/11 report which he had e-mailed as an attachment to the Saudis from his Hotmail address. Even I was shocked. He was, in effect, breaking the law as well as breaching CIA security protocol. Treasonable. But the smartphone, which was for his personal use, also contained all the e-mails sent by Charles Henke from that phone.

They are self-explanatory.

I wanted to pass what I had found to Deborah Jones, but I believe that Henke and another at the CIA were on to me very quickly. I don't know how. But they were.

Mum and Dad, I'll love you forever.

Do what you think is the right thing. I only wish I was there.

Love, peace and respect

John

X

Tears ran down Bill Hudson's face. Positioning the cursor over the second folder, he clicked it open.

The first file was the missing twenty-eight pages of

the Congressional Report that they'd already seen. The second was the CIA Fallback protocol.

'This is incredible,' Bill said. 'Is this what John died for?'

'Almost definitely,' said Sam.

They uncovered confidential encrypted e-mail contact between Charles Henke and Princess Hind al-Bassi. One message in particular excited all three of them more than the others. Charles Henke sent it from his Hotmail address on 6 July 2006, with the Fallback protocol attached. His message read simply, 'As requested, C.'

It had to mean Charles. He was feeding the Saudi princess, whose name was blacked out of the 9/11 report, highly secretive CIA documents about Al-Qaeda. It was now clear that Charles Henke's claim that John Hudson had been some patsy who'd come under the spell of a low-ranking CIA spy was an elaborate false trail. Henke was in cahoots with the enemy. And he was conducting his illegal activities away from his secure environment within Langley, on a smartphone, quite contrary to strict CIA regulations.

Deborah remembered speaking to Larry Coen about the CIA and how they conducted their business. Apparently each member of staff at Langley had two computers – one connected to classified systems, the other for Net surfing and sending unclassified e-mail. Most of the work of a CIA analyst would be carried out on the classified network. But if staff wanted to copy data to portable devices like BlackBerrys, proper authorization was required. Clearly, Henke was working to his own agenda.

'But why on earth would Henke leak such sensitive material?' Bill said.

'Money,' Sam said. 'We have information that Henke's wife is a regular gambler, losing tens of thousands, sometimes hundreds of thousands of dollars in Vegas. So he obviously needed money to fund his wife's ongoing habit and to pay her debts. And, of course, he has his own lifestyle to maintain.

'He lives in a plush colonial home in Bethesda, one of the best suburbs of Washington DC. Worth four million, conservative estimate. Also got a place in Georgetown. Perhaps worth six million.

'The opportunity to earn huge amounts of money occurred when he worked for a security firm before he was handed this plum CIA job. With Henke in charge, they landed a colossal contract with the Saudi oil ministry, which this al-Bassi woman's brother runs. There will have been a few juicy kickbacks there.'

Deborah looked first at Bill, and then at Sam. 'I think it's time to shake the tree.'

56

After a long strategy meeting at the *Herald*, Harry managed to get out of the newsroom just before three p.m. He drove straight to the Random Everglades Middle School on South Bayshore Drive. Rebecca and Andrew were both there outside the gates, along with a long line of glamorous mothers, nannies, the occasional father and scores of BMWs, Mercedes, Jeeps and other smart cars.

'So, what's the big deal?' Rebecca asked, strapping herself into the front passenger seat. 'You sounded stressed.'

Harry headed north along South Miami Avenue. 'I'll explain everything.' He took a right onto the Rickenbacker, paid the toll and sped across the bridge.

'Did you bring the ball?' Andrew asked, when they pulled up at Crandon Beach.

Harry got it from the trunk of his car and threw it

to his son, who quickly stripped to the waist in the blistering sun. 'Fifteen minutes, okay?' he shouted.

His son didn't waste any time showing off the tricks he'd learned at a soccer training camp.

Harry donned his shades and headed onto the beach with Rebecca. He told her that their relationship was no longer a secret, and also about the pressure he'd come under to stop the investigation, as well about as the blackmail threats.

They strolled slowly towards the ocean, to all intents and purposes a happy couple engrossed in each other.

Harry motioned for her to sit beside him on the hot white sand.

'I just want to get on with my life, Harry,' Rebecca said. 'I don't need this, any of it. All I care about is Andrew. His welfare. His future.'

Harry put his arm around her and whispered in her ear. 'This is the only way I can be sure that they won't monitor what I'm about to say. I don't know if my car is bugged but I do know that my home is bugged and my phone will have been bugged. That's why I'm using a friend's cellphone at the moment.'

'This is insane.'

'Yes, it is. And I haven't been thinking straight. This morning I spoke to my lawyer. His name is Arrie Molscher of Molscher and Leibowitz. I've decided to go to the feds. In an hour's time.'

'Are you sure you have thought this through?'

Harry had to stop for a moment so they could watch

Andrew attempt to keep the ball in the air for a couple of minutes, using both feet. He grinned at his parents as the ball finally dropped to the sand.

'If something happens to me,' Harry continued, giving a thumbs-up signal to his son, 'you and Andrew will be taken care of. You won't have to worry about money. All my investments, savings, bonds, they will be yours, Rebecca. When Andrew turns twenty-one, a trust fund kicks in.'

'You're starting to scare me, Harry. You don't really think this can happen, do you?'

'It's simply a precaution. Two hackers are dead, and some ex-CIA author who was helping Deborah apparently ended up killing himself. I want you and Andrew to stay with Arrie and his wife and family for the next month, until this is finished. I'll get the feds to relocate you if need be.'

'I don't want to be goddamn relocated. What's the matter with you?'

'This is not a game, Rebecca. I can't impress that on you enough. You either do as I say, or I'll take Andrew to Arrie's place myself.'

Rebecca broke away from him. 'What am I going to tell Andrew?'

'Tell him what I've told you. He's a smart kid. He'll understand. But tell him to keep quiet about it, okay?'

'Will you be given protective custody?'

'Who knows?'

Rebecca put her head in her hands and groaned.

'I don't have a choice anymore,' Harry said. 'The investigation is back up and running, but I seem to be the one in these people's sights. And I think they tend to shoot first.'

'How do we get there?'

'Arrie's driver will pick you up. If someone is following me I don't want them to know where you are. It's not far from here. And you'll have a cottage in the grounds, so you'll have complete privacy as well as security.'

'And you trust him?'

'Absolutely. But it's up to you. What do you say?'

'I'm frightened.'

Harry gazed down the beach towards his son who was still kicking the ball around as some Latinos wearing fluorescent Speedos swaggered by. 'Look after our boy. That's all I ask.'

57

Late afternoon, and the sky was burnt-orange when Nathan Stone cut the powerful twin-outboard engine of the cruiser two miles from Key Biscayne. It was nearly five p.m. He peered through his binoculars across the choppy waters at the waterfront mansion on South Mashta Drive, the upscale enclave where Cher used to live. The subject still wasn't home.

He scanned the frequencies used by the Miami-Dade police marine-patrol boats, by the DEA with their high-speed interceptor patrol boats, and by Customs. The drug smuggling gangs of south Florida were mainly based in Miami. Marijuana and cocaine from the Caribbean and Central and South America were smuggled up and down the Miami River with impunity, despite the best efforts of local law enforcement. But there was nothing doing today. Which was fine by Nathan.

'Where the fuck are you?' He put down his binoculars and entered a number on his cellphone.

The familiar voice answered, as he always did, after three rings. 'What's the problem?'

'I was going to ask you the same thing,' Nathan said. 'No sign of our guy. You've not lost him, have you?'

A few moments' silence before he spoke. 'Apparently, his car is stuck in a huge jam on Crandon Boulevard. Four-car smash.'

'Is he okay?'

'He wasn't involved. Hold on.' A beat. 'Yeah, I've just checked, the traffic has just started moving again. He should be with you in five minutes.'

Nathan enjoyed the cool salt-water spray on his face. He picked up the binoculars again. 'Outside security lights have just come on.'

'Sensor activated. He must've arrived home. That was quick.'

A few moments elapsed before the lights came on in the house.

'I'll let you know when I'm done.' Nathan ended the call, placing the cellphone in his back pocket. The subject headed out onto the terrace, drinking a glass of white wine.

Nathan focused in on his subject, the powerful Steiner military binoculars picking up the dark shadows under his eyes. Draining his glass, the man turned around and went back inside.

Nathan checked his watch. It was 4.59 p.m.

Not long now.

Through the binoculars he could see the man was now sitting on a sofa, watching TV.

Nathan felt his pulse accelerate. He took out his cellphone and rang a number.

He was calling another cellphone, which he'd taped to a copper gas pipe in the basement, a pipe which he'd deliberately filed until it had fractured.

A moment later a thunderous explosion tore through the mansion. Giant flames licked the Miami sky, then secondary explosions reduced the house to a blazing shell within seconds.

58

The close-up TV shots from news choppers showed the smoldering remains of the waterfront mansion. Fire crews were still at work, using water from the bay. A blonde female reporter stood outside the gates as the sun set in the background and, as if she were doing the weather forecast, intoned that this was a 'terrible accident for a truly gifted newspaperman'.

'Question is,' said Sam, 'how much do you want this story? Is it really worth all this?'

Deborah switched off the TV. 'You're damn right it is,' she said.

There had been a somber meeting in the *Herald* conference room the day after Harry's death, and now Rafferty and Deborah had moved to Sam's office.

'I'll switch it onto the speakers so everyone can hear the conversation,' Sam said, pressing a button on his phone.

Deborah's mouth felt dry. 'Well, here goes.'

He answered after four rings. 'Yeah, who's this?' His voice was low and gravelly.

'Mr Henke, it's Deborah Jones of the *Miami Herald*. Can we talk?'

'Make it brief, Miss Jones. I've got an important meeting in fifteen minutes.'

'I'd like to talk again about the secret documents we uncovered.'

Henke sighed. 'We have been through all this already. There is, as I told you, an ongoing internal investigation which is reaching a critical juncture, and—'

'I remember what you said. However, we have unearthed further sensitive documents.'

Henke went quiet.

'Mr Henke, can you explain to me why you sent sensitive CIA strategy documents to a Saudi princess implicated in the funding of some of those involved in the September 11 attacks?'

'I have no idea what you're talking about. Look, why don't you—'

'Mr Henke, with all due respect, we need some answers. Otherwise we will have no choice but to go straight to the Senate Intelligence Committee. And then there is the question of the deaths of John Hudson and Harry Donovan, not to mention that of Richard Turner.'

'Don't ever threaten me, Miss Jones,' Henke said. 'And don't fuck with me. You have no idea what you're dealing with. No idea at all.'

And he put down the phone.

'There's someone I think we're forgetting about,' Sam said, breaking the stunned silence in his office.

Deborah nodded. 'The princess?'

'Absolutely. She is attending a function in West Palm Beach tonight,' Sam said.

'How do you know that?' Rafferty asked.

'I still have my sources,' replied Sam, with a grin. 'Princess Hind al-Bassi is one of the biggest patrons of the Norton Museum of Art in West Palm Beach. And I have the last remaining press ticket!'

Ed Rafferty frowned. 'You're going to ask Deborah to do this?'

'No. This is a job for Larry Coen. We've got the story, but we need to know what this princess has to say for herself. Does that sound okay to you, Deborah?'

'Sorry, Sam, but this is my investigation. It has been from the beginning. Now, while I appreciate that you want to protect me, if anyone's going to ask questions face to face, it's going to be me.'

59

Nathan Stone lay on top of his bed, blowing smoke rings, killing time. He was waiting for the call. In the next room, the raised voices of a gay couple having a blazing argument about the spilled amyl nitrate were keeping him vaguely entertained.

He heard a van pull up outside the main entrance to the motel. He got to his feet and looked out of the window. A heavy-set Hispanic delivery guy stepped out of a Fed-Ex delivery van with a clipboard and a bulky rectangular-shaped parcel. Then he set off up the stairs.

Nathan opened the door and waited.

'Robert Jackson?' The delivery man was puffing slightly.

'That's me.' Nathan signed under the false name and checked the man's badge. 'Thanks, Ramon.' He took the parcel and handed over a ten-dollar note. 'Good service, man.'

'Okay, sir, thank you. Have a nice day.'

'You too.' Nathan forced a smile.

Back inside, Nathan locked the door, took his Swiss army knife from his back pocket and ripped open the package. It contained two smaller packets. He felt his heart beginning to thump faster.

Inside the first parcel was a police regulation belt, nightstick, flashlight, badge, Taser and 9mm Glock 27 with ammo.

'And what have we got here?' he said to himself, opening the second packet.

He took out a neatly folded bespoke dark blue police uniform and tie, as well as a shiny gold badge – with fake name and number – and black police-issue shoes.

Nathan took a long shower, shaved, then carefully applied some skin-tone make-up to conceal the marks from the burn wounds on his face. He buttoned up his shirt and tightened the knot of his tie. Checking his reflection in the bathroom mirror, he was pleased to find that he looked just the part.

Then he opened a locked drawer in his bedside cabinet and pulled out a small plastic bag of white powder.

Nathan chopped up three long raggedy lines on the cabinet, rolled up a twenty-dollar bill, and snorted the lot.

60

Deborah stood in front of a full-length bedroom mirror at McNally's Fisher Island home, admiring the ivory satin dress he'd picked up earlier from her condo. Her heart was pounding hard.

Sam popped his head round the door gingerly before entering her room. Then he shut the door quietly behind him.

Deborah smiled. 'So, what do you think?'

'Are you serious? You look fantastic.'

Sam stepped forward and wrapped his arms around her waist. Then he pulled her close and kissed her lips. It felt good.

'I'm gonna be sashaying beside some of the wealthiest people in south Florida, and I want to look the part. Besides, if I want to get up close to the princess I'll need more than a press ticket.'

Sam seemed to sense how nervous she was. 'Look,

you don't have to go through with this. If you are having second thoughts, don't be—'

'I'm fine, really.'

'Really?'

'Yes, really.'

'It wouldn't be any problem to get a replacement reporter up there.'

'I know that, Sam, but, as I said before, this is *my* investigation.' Deborah sighed. 'Look, there is one thing that's still bugging me. Gnawing away at me.'

'What's that?'

'Sam, this whole lone conspiracy theory just seems too goddamn neat.'

'How?'

'Think about it. Everything we have is pointing to Henke, albeit with Simmons perhaps in a supporting role, right?'

Sam nodded

'Are we really to believe that this is all the work of Henke? That he's the lone crazy and that no one else within Langley, or other agencies, is involved in this, or even aware of it at a strategic level? Is this really plausible?'

'You don't believe this stops at Henke?'

'How can it? I believe this conspiracy runs deeper. Which poses even more fundamental questions. Does no one in the Pentagon know about this? And if not, why not? And what about the Saudis' General Intelligence Directorate? Are they involved? They have to be.'

Sam shut her up with another kiss. 'Let's leave those

questions for another day. Then we can open this whole thing out.'

Deborah smiled and picked up her matching handbag from an easy chair and tucked it under her arm. Inside she'd crammed her tape recorder, cellphone, notepad, pens, lipstick and mascara.

'Once this story is done and dusted,' he said, 'we're going to sit down and talk about us, for a change. No more fleeting lunches, or dinners on the run. I want us to be a real couple.'

'I'm going to hold you to that,' Deborah said.

The traffic was heavy. Deborah's headlights strafed the freeway ahead. She glanced in her rear-view mirror and saw McNally's SUV right behind her.

As the miles rolled by, the night sky over south Florida inky black, Deborah wondered how the evening would unfold. Would she be able to get near the princess?

She tuned in her radio to a classical station and was pleased to find some soothing Brahms.

After an hour-long drive north, Deborah headed off the freeway and negotiated the dimly lit streets of downtown West Palm Beach, the car's satellite navigation system guiding her to the destination.

The Norton Museum of Art was fringed by palms. She pulled up in the parking lot behind the museum and checked in her rear-view mirror. McNally had parked directly behind her.

She got out, locked her car and waved towards McNally. She couldn't see his face behind the tinted windows, but he flashed his headlights anyway.

61

Deborah was directed through the museum lobby to a futuristic three-storey atrium. A string quartet played in the background. Scores of guests chatted noisily. Some of them were sitting on the cantilevered spiral staircase, sipping champagne, nibbling canapés.

Deborah waited for a moment on the terrazzo floor with its cracked ice-blue pattern until a Hispanic waiter approached with a tray of drinks. She selected a glass of grapefruit juice.

'Excuse me,' she said, 'I'm wondering if the princess has arrived?'

The waiter gave a vacant smile. 'The princess?'

'The guest of honor.'

'Oh yeah, sure. Right. Seen her about fifteen minutes ago. Don't know where she is now, though. Probably getting the VIP tour.'

Deborah looked around at the throng, mostly

middle-aged, heavily tanned and immaculately coiffured donors who were dressed to kill. The heady mix of perfume and power hung in the air.

Deborah lingered by herself for a few minutes before drifting out to the west courtyard. She drew glances from a couple of guests before she headed into the Pavilion Room, just off the atrium. A handful of younger guests mingled under an aqua-blue and green glass ceiling. It overlooked a reflecting pool and an isle of palm trees.

Noticing a sign for the galleries, she ambled towards the collection of late-nineteenth- and early-twentieth-century American paintings, sculptures and drawings.

Apart from a bored-looking museum official, the room was empty.

Deborah moved on to the Contemporary and European galleries. No one was there either. Where the hell was the princess? Outside the prestigious Chinese collection were two burly men of Middle Eastern appearance, both in dark suits. One was muttering into a cellphone. He looked up as Deborah approached a rather timid-looking female museum official.

'Excuse me,' Deborah said, 'is it okay to see the collection?'

The woman gave a wan smile. 'Private viewing, I'm afraid. Try again in fifteen minutes.'

The bodyguards moved to block Deborah's path, expressionless.

Suddenly the gallery doors opened and the Director

of the Museum stepped out, followed by more body-guards. She thanked a slight woman with dark brown eyes who was swathed in a long white silk dress.

At that moment, time stood still.

Deborah quickly switched her cellphone to micro-phone mode. 'Excuse me, Princess al-Bassi.' Her voice was not as steady as she would have liked. The body-guards eyed her suspiciously but didn't move. 'Just a moment of your time, please. I'm Deborah Jones of the *Miami Herald*. May I ask you a question?'

The princess smiled at Deborah. 'Yes, of course. I'd be delighted.'

'Our newspaper is about to conclude an investigation into alleged links between a senior member of American intelligence and yourself, Princess al-Bassi.'

The princess frowned. 'I beg your pardon?'

'We have evidence that you are mentioned in the twenty-eight censored pages of the 9/11 report. But we are looking for clarification on another point, if I may?'

The princess, stony-faced, said nothing.

'How long have you known the Deputy Director of the CIA, Charles Henke?'

'I'm sorry. I think you must have mistaken me for someone else.'

'With respect, Princess al-Bassi, is it possible that Charles Henke's previous role at Platinum Security Solutions was the reason he decided to send you highly confidential documents pertaining to national security?'

'Would you let me pass, please? We have nothing to discuss.'

'I think we do, princess. I should like you to explain your links to the September 11 attackers, and why it is that you continue to fund jihadists in mosques across Afghanistan and the Middle East.'

The museum director flushed crimson. 'Please escort this young lady off the premises,' she snapped to an assistant. 'Now!'

The bodyguards stepped forward and each of them grabbed one of Deborah's arms. But before they could march her away she managed one last question. 'Is it true that you continue to fund Al-Qaeda to this day, Princess al-Bassi?'

Deborah's feet did not touch the ground until she was dumped outside. A well-heeled couple getting out of a silver Daimler looked vaguely surprised but took little notice.

Deborah was seething. But what other result could she have expected? At least she had managed to have the confrontation, and it was all recorded on her cell-phone.

As she unlocked her SUV, she waved at McNally's car which was still parked behind her.

She was about to put the key in the ignition when she felt cold steel pressed against the back of her neck.

62

Sam Goldberg paced the thick carpet in his office for the hundredth time.

'I don't like it,' he said to Frank Callaghan. 'Why hasn't Thomas called in?'

'Sam, just relax.'

'He said he'd call every ten minutes. I've not heard from him for twenty-two minutes. He's not answering his goddamn cellphone. And neither is Deborah. I can't believe I authorized this. I must've lost my mind.'

He stared at the Stygian darkness of Biscayne, car lights moving slowly across the causeway. Then he had an idea and reached for his phone.

He waited a few moments before a woman's voice answered. 'The Norton Museum.'

'Good evening. My name's Sam Goldberg. I'm managing editor of the *Miami Herald*.'

'Good evening, sir. How may I help you?'

'Who's in charge of security for this evening?'

'Hold one minute, sir.' Sam had to listen to some discreet Vivaldi before a man's voice came on. 'Ron Leach, security manager. You're calling from the *Herald*?'

'Yes, Mr Leach. One of my reporters is among the guests this evening, and I was wondering—'

'Your reporter was thrown out, Mr Goldberg. Harassing one of our top patrons is never a good move.'

Sam winced. 'I see. Listen, she arrived in a black SUV, and there's a guy, Thomas McNally, driving a pale blue SUV, who's supposed to be keeping an eye on her. But I'm not getting any reply on his phone. Can you do me a favor and check outside to see if everything's all right?'

'You're kidding me, right?'

'Do I sound like I'm joking? Look, Miss Jones has been threatened recently over an investigation she's working on. Can you help me out? I'm asking you nicely. Please check that the vehicles are there, along with their drivers.'

Leach gave a theatrical sigh. 'We've got a lot on our plate tonight, as you can imagine, but I'll get one of my men to take a look. A black SUV and a pale blue SUV you say? License plates?'

'I'm sorry, I don't know.'

'Okay, I'll call you back in five minutes.'

The minutes dragged as Sam wandered up and down the office.

'There could be a perfectly innocent reason, Sam,' Frank said. 'Look, it's probably a glitch in the cellphone network.'

'In West Palm Beach? It's hardly Nowheresville.'

Frank said nothing.

'I'm just thinking, what if the psycho who attacked Deborah has got to her?'

'Don't go there, Sam.'

'I authorized the goddamn thing. But my gut instinct was to send Larry Coen out there tonight. After all that's happened.'

'So why didn't you?'

Sam groaned. 'Because she insisted on going. I thought it would be fine with Thomas there.' He closed his eyes. 'How can I have been so dumb?'

'You did the right thing. You let her continue with the investigation but made sure someone was there for her.'

'But he isn't, is he?'

'You don't know that.'

Sam jabbed his chest. 'I feel it here. Something is not right.'

Frank rubbed his eyes. It had been a long day.

Suddenly Sam's desk phone rang and he switched the speakers on.

'Goldberg,' he said.

'Ron Leach at the Norton Museum. My guy checked over the two vehicles, which are still, as we speak, parked in the west parking lot of the museum. Everything's fine.'

'Did your guy check if there was anyone in the cars?'

'He tapped on the windows of both, but there was no reply. I guess they're still in the reception.'

'I asked you to make sure the two people were with their vehicles.'

'Mr Goldberg, there was nothing amiss. No windows broken, no signs of forced entry. The dark tinted glass meant he couldn't see inside.'

'This is a goddamn emergency,' Sam snapped. 'Break the windows if you have to. Do you understand me? And call the goddamn cops.'

'Sir, I think you're overreacting.'

'Listen to me, Ron. If my reporter was thrown out of the reception, where the hell is she now?'

'I don't have time to babysit your people, Mr Goldberg. Now I'm going to hang up. I've got work to do.'

The line went dead.

'Great,' Sam said.

'Hang on, hang on.' Frank frowned, then started clicking his fingers as if trying to remember a name. 'West Palm Beach, we did an article about a police chief there, couple of years back.'

'And?'

'Diane Mosley. She was the first African-American member of the West Palm Beach Police Department way back in the 1980s when she joined up, and she worked her way to the top.'

'You want me to call her up?'

'It might sound desperate, but you never know.'

'You want me to tell her that a young black journalist could be in danger, is that your line?'

Frank held up his palms. 'I wouldn't put it so crudely. But just give it to her straight.'

'Worth a try.' Sam pulled up the website of the West Palm Beach Police Department, located at 600 Banyan Boulevard. He punched in the phone number and waited.

A gruff voice answered. 'West Palm Beach Police Department, how can I help?'

'Good evening. My name's Sam Goldberg, managing editor of the *Miami Herald*. I need to speak to your chief urgently.'

'I'm sorry, she's in a community meeting.'

'This is urgent, or I wouldn't be making the call. I really need to speak to her. Right now.'

'Gimme a minute.'

'Thank you.'

Less than a minute later, a woman's voice came on. 'Yes?' She sounded irritable already.

'I'm very sorry to interrupt your meeting, but I need your help. I have an investigative reporter, Deborah Jones—'

'I've read her work.'

Sam quickly explained the situation.

'Ah hah,' Chief Mosley said. 'You thought that because I'm a black woman I'd jump. Listen to me. My officers are far too busy to go heading off on some crazy wild-goose chase, just because some journalist is not returning her cellphone messages or some security guy has switched off his phone. Please don't waste my time again.'

63

The man's hand covered Deborah's mouth, pressing her head back, as a gum-chewing uniformed security man wandered around the car.

I'm in here, she wanted to scream.

She knew what every woman was told. Always try and make a run for it. But she couldn't.

So she sat there, knife at her neck, ice in her veins.

The man whispered in her ear. 'You will die if there's any noise or any sudden movement. So be a good girl. I like good girls.'

Deborah stared wide-eyed through the privacy glass as the security guard spoke into his radio and then walked away. Where the hell was McNally?

The man relaxed his grip round her neck. 'Slowly, very slowly, I want you to put your key in the ignition. Then we will drive off. Now, do you think you can do that?'

Deborah nodded, tasting salty tears.

'Okay, nice and easy, I want you to take I-95 and head south.'

Deborah took a deep breath and did what she was told. The knife was removed from against her neck and the man slumped back in the rear seat, where he began to hum softly to himself.

Deborah took a wrong turning in West Palm Beach and skirted past the regenerated section of downtown, City Place. 'Let's not do anything silly,' the man said. 'Take the freeway.'

'Sorry.'

City Place modeled itself on a European town, full of fine architecture, beautiful fountains, sidewalk cafes, restaurants and bars. Deborah saw a couple of police officers drinking coffees, leaning on their cruisers. She wondered if she shouldn't just risk it, come to a sudden halt and jump out.

She was doing around thirty miles per hour. She weighed the options but her nerve failed her.

Instead, she took a left and was soon heading along Okeechobee Boulevard. There was the sign up ahead for I-95 S.

She'd lost the moment.

Deborah glanced in the rear-view mirror and saw the man smiling back at her. She felt sick. 'Where are we going?'

He smiled and said nothing.

'I said where are we—'

'Due south.'

'Due south, right. Where exactly? Miami?'

'Maybe.'

Was this how it was to end? Driving to a remote location so he could kill her? Deborah tried to act calm, driving sensibly, not breaking any speed limit, but inside her stomach was churning, her mind was in free fall.

The miles rolled by. Past Greenacres, Delray Beach, Coral Springs and Fort Lauderdale. The lights of the oncoming cars were dazzling.

'Get onto the South Dixie Highway, and then onto the turnpike,' the man said.

He wanted her to ignore Miami and head on south, deeper and deeper into southeast Florida.

64

'Sorry to bother you again, Mr Leach. It's Sam Goldberg.'

'I appreciate that you are worried, Mr Goldberg, but we've already checked the two vehicles. There's nothing amiss.'

'Please check again. I'm begging you.'

'What the hell is—'

'Just do it, goddamn it. Look, if everything's fine I'll owe you one.'

'You people are nuts.'

A few excruciating minutes elapsed. Frank and Sam sat in silence, fearing the worst. Eventually Leach came back on the line, breathing hard. 'Mr Goldberg, sir?'

'Yeah, what is it?'

'The guy in the pale blue BMW SUV...He's bleeding. Badly. His throat's been cut. My people have just called the cops and the paramedics, and they're on their way.'

'Is he dead or alive?'

'I don't know.'

Sam felt sick. 'You don't know? What about the other vehicle?'

'There is no black SUV, sir.'

'What the fuck are you talking about? I thought your guy said he'd checked over both vehicles earlier. Did you or did you not tell me that?'

'Yes, I did tell you that. But there is no black SUV there now.'

'Listen to me,' Sam said. 'Tell the cops they're looking for a black BMW SUV, vehicle registered to Andrea McNally, Fisher Island, Miami. You got that?'

'McNally . . . Black SUV. Leave it with me. Look, I'm really sorry, I thought you were—'

'Forget it. Just pass on those details, and get my friend to the hospital.'

'Hold on.' It sounded as if Leach had covered the mouthpiece with his hand. Then he came back clearly on the line. 'The guy who checked out the two SUVs, he's just told me this moment that someone spotted a uniformed cop speaking to the driver of the pale blue SUV in the parking lot just over an hour ago. I'm watching the footage on our cameras now.'

'Cop?'

'Looks like a cop.'

'Jesus. Okay, thanks for that.'

Sam's heart was pounding as he hung up. He took a few moments to gather his thoughts before he dialed the number for West Palm Beach police, and asked to be transferred to Chief Mosley. She was on the line within seconds.

'I thought I'd told you that I couldn't divert resources away from—'

'Just listen to me. A man's throat has been cut, and one of my reporters is now AWOL, perhaps kidnapped by some crazy fuck, we don't really know. Now I need your help on this. And I need it now.'

'Excuse me?'

'Are you deaf? Check with your guys on the ground. In the west parking lot of the Norton Museum of Art a friend of mine has just had his throat cut.'

'Yeah, yeah . . . I've just this second had confirmation of that. Look, I'm sorry . . .'

'As I mentioned earlier, we believe one of our reporters, Deborah Jones, may have been kidnapped by someone dressed as a cop.'

'You've got to be kidding me.'

'I've just talked to the security guy at the museum. It's all on camera. We believe this is the man who threatened Miss Jones and put me in hospital, just a few days ago in Miami.'

'Okay – you got any details of the vehicle Deborah Jones is driving?'

'It's a black BMW SUV, license plate registered to McNally, Fisher Island, Miami.'

'Okay, here's what I'm going to do. I'll get the helicopter unit on it, straight away, and put out an APB.'

'She could be anywhere.'

'We'll try and lock onto the GPS. Look, Mr Goldberg, I can only apologize, but—'

'Just make sure it's done, chief.'

Sam hung up, gripped by a feeling of anger at his own stupidity but also by a sense of dread at the events unfolding.

65

Deborah stared at the turnpike toll-booths up ahead, and joined one of the long queues. She was desperately trying to figure out an escape plan. Was this the time to make a break for it? This could be her last chance, after all.

'Not a fucking word or movement out of place, you hear?' She felt the tip of the blade at her throat.

Deborah wound down the window and smiled at the overweight white man chewing gum inside the toll-booth. He stared at her for a few moments, as if sensing that something was wrong. 'You okay, lady?' he asked. 'You been crying?'

'I'm fine.'

'You don't *look* fine.'

'Just bad news, that's all.'

'I see.' He took a long hard look at the man in the back. 'You take care now.'

She paid the toll meekly. Then she drove on in silence, blinking away the tears.

'Take exit one for Florida City.'

A short while later, Deborah was entering Homestead, just over thirty miles southwest of Miami. It was a town of around thirty thousand residents, which had been devastated by Hurricane Andrew in 1992. It nestled between Biscayne National Park to the east and the Everglades to the west. She was driving through the downtown area and the man began telling her which way to go. Past city hall and the clock outside, then past a Baptist church, doubling back past the Redland Hotel and a quaint antique shop. Then she felt his breath on her ear.

'Take a right turn.' Obviously he knew the area well. 'Then we're going to head due west, okay?'

Deborah's stomach churned while the sleepy town disappeared from sight as they headed out along the State Road 9336 and the southern outskirts of Homestead disappeared from sight. A mile later they were passing motels and tiny diners in the small town of Florida City.

They drove on, leaving the town and the last remnants of civilization behind them. The road merged and they were on the Ingraham Highway, driving past fields, the occasional farm enveloped by the suffocating darkness of the Everglades.

The SUV's headlights disturbed some pelicans and ibises which took flight into the starry south Florida sky.

They passed the visitor center of the Everglades National Park.

Deborah had hiked and camped several times in the subtropical wetland prairie. It was made up of large tree islands – tropical hardwood hammocks – and small shrubby islands called bay heads, interspersed with mangrove forests, swamp, and gumbo limbo trees, half-submerged in the mostly fresh or brackish water that teemed with alligators and snakes.

It was a perfect place for someone to disappear.

The River of Grass.

Deborah thought of her father, probably sleeping at home in Jackson, her mother watching a late-night film and sipping her cocoa. But most of all she thought of Sam, almost certainly in his office and out of his mind with worry.

Suddenly the road became bumpy, the SUV lurching from side to side, making her feel nauseous.

'You gonna do to me what you did to John Hudson, huh?'

The man said nothing, but his eyes glinted in the rear-view mirror.

'So who sent you? Was it Charlie Henke? Well, we're on to him. And he's going down. Trust me on that.'

Still the man said nothing.

The road was now fringing the sawgrass and twisted mangroves in the water, where cottonmouth snakes lurked. She smelled the damp, fecund aroma of the swamps, the hardwood hammocks, live oaks, pawpaws and cypresses.

Deborah decided that it was time. She floored the

accelerator. The SUV roared and lurched along the pitch-black road. Tears flooded her eyes.

'Slow down, you fucking idiot,' the man shouted.

Deborah turned the wheel sharp left and then right. She undid her safety belt. And then she started laughing.

Deborah was going to go down fighting. She hurtled along the road that ran through a wetland restoration area. She smashed through the gate and drove on. The old borrow canal was running alongside the road on the north and west. Small cypress trees were dotted all around.

The man's arm was around her throat, his knife pressed to her neck. She felt warm blood.

'You gonna die, bitch.'

Deborah veered to the right. The SUV flipped over and plunged into the dark waters of the Everglades. Muddied water flooded in as the airbag jammed her tight against the steering wheel. Shock spread through her body. For some reason she hadn't expected it to be so cold, knowing the Florida winters were relatively mild. She began to choke. The tannin water stung her eyes, ears and nose. The car was under water, sinking softly into the mud and silt.

Deborah was trapped.

Her dress was wrapped round her face and she ripped part of it off. For a few desperate seconds she struggled to get her bearings. She was swallowing water and bits of leaves and mud in the pitch black.

Above her the man was locked into his seat by his

belt, looming like a crazed gargoyle, slashing at her through the water, missing by inches.

Deborah struggled to hold her breath and managed not to scream as something brushed past her. It was a snake.

A cottonmouth.

She was trapped by the airbag. And, despite her efforts, she couldn't at first get free. But miraculously, inch by inch, she finally began to extricate herself. Straining, she managed to stretch out a free hand to the floor and felt inside her bag. Her purse, lipstick and . . . It was out of reach. Then she had it. Her nail file, to burst the bag.

The car lurched in the mud, and the nail file was lost in the sediment and water.

Deborah knew she had only seconds to live. Her lungs were full to bursting. She ripped wildly at the bag and it burst in a watery explosion.

She leaned over and tried to open the passenger-seat window, but it wouldn't budge. She banged at the windows, but nothing happened.

All of a sudden she felt the man on top of her.

He was free.

One hand was round her throat; the other still held the knife. She jolted at a searing pain in her neck. And again – this time in her shoulder.

And she swallowed more murky water.

Her lungs were ready to explode. She felt herself drifting away.

Deborah opened her eyes one last time and saw the knife coming down at her.

Summoning every ounce of strength in her exhausted body she launched herself at her attacker. She tore into his face and eyes with her nails, piercing the skin and flesh. She felt exultant to see his astonishment and rage. And his blood.

Frantically, she clawed herself further up to the top of the SUV, away from him.

In a split second Deborah noticed that the rear of the car, which was pointing upwards, still held an air pocket. Lashing out with her leg, she caught the man right on his windpipe and pushed out to gulp in the precious air.

A few inches from her feet, he scrabbled to catch hold of her. But she could see that he was stuck and was flailing about in the near-darkness of the muddy water.

She saw bubbles come from his mouth. And then there was no movement.

Everything below Deborah's chin was under water. Her feet were planted on the headrests of the rear seats. She began to shiver uncontrollably.

The back of her head was jammed against the rear window. She was too scared to move, in case the SUV sank deeper into the mud. Tears and blood and mud smeared her vision. Dead leaves and bits of rotten branches floated in the black water.

Suddenly she was in total darkness. The light from the full moon, which had reflected into the upturned rear window of the SUV, was gone. She closed her eyes and thought of Sam, and of cloudless skies. She thought of children. That was what she wanted. More than anything.

Deborah opened her eyes as she felt the water beginning to rise. She craned her neck a half-inch as the water started to seep into her mouth. She tasted the mud and sediment, mixed with her own blood.

The water was rising. How was that possible?

Then a ripple in the water against her cheeks. She heard birds taking flight. And a distant low drone. It got louder. And closer. And then a brilliant beam of light shone down.

A helicopter was directly above her, the rotor blades causing a downdraft and whipping the water into her mouth.

Deborah thought her heart was going to burst. Tears streamed down her face. She heard voices. And sirens blaring.

66

At the end of her hospital bed Deborah's father and mother were sitting quiet, smiling at her. Immaculate as always.

'You're okay, honey,' her mother said. 'Momma's here. They say you're gonna do just fine.'

Sam leaned over and kissed her, tears spilling down his cheeks. 'Welcome back, darling. You're safe.' His beautiful world-weary blue eyes stared down at her. 'No one's gonna hurt you any more.'

Deborah stroked his hair and smiled. 'You promise?'

Sam nodded. 'I promise. I never thought I'd see you again.'

'You don't get rid of me that easily.'

The following afternoon, after a deep nightmare-free sleep, Deborah could feel her strength returning. She was more alert. She sat up in her bed. And she asked Sam for her laptop.

67

The next evening, just as they were about to go to press, Sam was sitting peacefully in a chair beside Deborah's bed when his cellphone rang.

'Goldberg,' he said, rubbing his eyes.

'Sam, it's Eddie. We got a problem with Deborah's story.'

'What are you talking about? This has been past Byron, and he said it's fine.'

'The CIA's lawyers have lodged a last-minute bid to stop publication of tomorrow's *Miami Herald*.'

'You got to be kidding me!'

'Byron said the judge is considering it at this moment. We're expecting to hear back within the hour.'

'This is bullshit, Eddie.'

'I know.'

'Okay, keep me posted.'

After the fire of energy that had consumed Deborah

when she'd been working up the Henke story, this news drained all the life from her.

She lay back on her starched white pillow and gazed blankly at the ceiling.

Ninety minutes later Sam's phone rang again, jolting Deborah awake.

'Yeah, talk to me, Eddie,' Sam said, grim-faced.

'The judge has just delivered his ruling.'

Sam looked at Deborah who stared back, her eyes heavy.

'Sam . . . Sam, the judge has ruled that it's in the national interest this story is not suppressed. He quoted the First Amendment which protects freedom of speech and freedom of the press.'

Deborah didn't have to be told that the news was good. And she sat up suddenly.

'Have we started printing?'

'Two minutes ago. They're already coming off the presses. And the story's gonna make international headlines tomorrow. So buckle up.'

Sam laughed out loud. 'Tell Byron he did good.'

'No, Sam, *you* did good. And Deborah. Tell her from me to get well soon. And I don't want to see her back in the newsroom for a goddamn month.'

68

Late the following morning, after a dreamless sleep, a nurse handed Deborah the first edition of the *Herald*. The headline on the front read: 'Renegade CIA boss: power, corruption and lies.' Deborah's byline and photo were attached to the story, which carried on to pages three, four, five and six.

It outlined in minute detail the crazy, corrupt world of Charles Henke and his psychopathic buddy Nathan Stone, and the devastating links with the reclusive Saudi princess. Miami-Dade's Chief Medical Examiner Brent Simmons was also revealed to have CIA links. He had mysteriously disappeared from Miami without giving any notice.

But it didn't end there.

They proved that Princess al-Bassi had escaped justice. Flight plans obtained by the *Herald* showed that her Gulfstream jet had left Palm Beach airport at 2.43 a.m., only hours after the confrontation with Deborah. The princess had been unable or unwilling to answers questions about her role in the 9/11 attacks. She was now living at her forty-two-bedroom mansion on the outskirts of Riyadh, protected by the might of the Saudi government.

However, the whereabouts of Charles Henke were unknown. Some reports suggested that he too was living in Riyadh at the behest of the Saudis, others that he had fled the country and was living in Brazil. Neither the Pentagon nor the CIA acknowledged the existence of the protocol, and both institutions claimed 'national security had not been jeopardized'. Moreover, they said that 'more robust safeguards' had been put in place to ensure a 'better flow of information' at the highest levels of the agency.

No evidence of a highly sophisticated network was unearthed.

Early in the afternoon the Jackson Memorial Hospital was under siege by the world's media. Everyone wanted a picture of the investigative journalist who'd pieced together the whole extraordinary story.

But Deborah wasn't interested.

People had died as a result of her investigation. Good people. And McNally was still on the critical list, even though he was out of intensive care.

Deborah was allowed to make her escape via a side door where Sam was waiting. She asked him to drive her to

Woodlawn Park Cemetery. Three former Cuban presidents were buried there. She still felt unsteady on her feet and was happy to have Sam's arm around her.

The inscription on John Hudson's alabaster headstone read:

'For our beloved son who believed in the truth: rest in peace'.

Only by the grace of God and her own good fortune had Deborah herself been spared.

She bent down and arranged the fresh lilies lying on the ground. 'Rest in peace, John,' she said.

As they strolled back out of the cemetery Deborah felt a strange mixture of sadness and elation, combined with profound mental exhaustion. She needed to get away from it all. Somewhere no one could bother them. No phones. No e-mails. No hassle. No nothing. Just peace.

'I'm not going back to the office,' Sam said, as if reading her thoughts. 'Not for a while.'

'You got any plans?'

'You wanna fly off tonight to Barbados?'

Deborah just smiled, tears in her eyes.

'There's something I want to say. Something I should've said a long time ago.'

'And what's that?'

'Deborah, I am nothing without you. And I've been a fool not telling you that. I always seem to have had some excuse for why I haven't committed more to you. Frankly, I'm at a loss to explain my behavior. The thing is . . . I need you. What I guess I'm trying to say is, Deborah, will you—'

'Yes,' she said, before he'd even finished his sentence.

'You don't know what I'm going to ask yet.'

'It doesn't matter. The answer is still yes.'

Sam smiled, his fond gaze confirming to her that she'd found the only man who understood and loved her.

'The answer will always be yes.'

They walked out of the cemetery, holding hands, as a burnt-orange sunset blanketed the quietest corner of Little Havana. Deborah felt the warmth of the last rays of the unforgiving Miami sun on her skin, and heard the merest sound of salsa music hanging in the warm night breeze.

Epilogue

Three days later, when the story had come off the front pages, a Learjet registered to a front company, Rossington Foundation of Palm Beach, Florida, swooped low over the scrub pines and fields of tobacco in rural Virginia on the banks of the York River. It landed at Camp Peary – also known as 'The Farm'. Six men and their bodyguards disembarked and made their way in a fleet of SUVs parked on the edge of the runway to an underground office.

The 9000-acre wooded site was officially referred to as the Armed Forces Experimental Training Activity, under the auspices of the Department of Defense, but it was widely viewed as a covert CIA training facility.

Armed guards patrolled the eight-foot-high barbed-wire fence.

None of the men spoke until they were safely underground.

*   *   *

At the same time, two hours' drive north, a removals truck with untraceable plates and with four men inside snaked its way around one of Washington's finest suburbs, Bethesda, the driver checking occasionally in the side mirror for any tail. The satellite navigation system on the driver's dashboard indicated that he should take a left, then a right.

A few minutes later the vehicle was guided to the only empty mansion on the block. In the middle of the newly mown lawn was a For Sale sign.

The driver reversed into the driveway. Then his three colleagues, dressed in matching dark blue uniforms and carrying duct tape, a toolbox and various cardboard boxes, got out and let themselves into the house owned by Charles Woodrow Henke.

Once inside, they got to work.

Using wiring diagrams, the senior man traced the cabling down into the cellar and another member of the group opened the toolbox. He unpacked the imaging equipment and meticulously scanned the stone floor. The three-dimensional images on the monitor were conclusive.

Fifteen minutes later they had uncovered a secret basement, as they'd been told they would. It contained two laptops wrapped in plastic, sitting on a desk. They were taken away in a box.

Late in the afternoon, after the basement had been stripped bare, including all wiring, the four-man team entered the Lamoura Tower in downtown Bethesda,

HQ of Lamoura Telecommunications. They rode the service elevator to the sixth floor and walked through a maze of corridors until they got to Room 614A.

The computer specialist – the youngest in the group – punched in the seven-digit access code. The door opened to reveal a massive room that contained around a dozen cabinets, including servers, routers and an industrial-size air-conditioner.

Two floors above, high-speed fiber-optic circuits were laid out on the eighth floor and ran down to the seventh floor where they connected to routers. But to monitor the information going through the circuits was some highly advanced circuitry inside a grey cabinet in this sixth-floor room.

The men crouched down. Stenciled in black on the front of the cabinet were the words 'Property of the US Government'.

The computer man pressed his thumb on the fingerprint-recognition panel at the side, which duly clicked and opened the cabinet. Inside were the stand-alone traffic analyzers that collected network and customer-usage information.

Then he flicked a switch, which routed the information back to a similar facility in downtown Seattle, which in turn fed back to the offices of the Security Intelligence Branch of the CIA.

The men left the building by a side entrance.

* * *

The basement office in Camp Peary smelled of stale coffee and donuts. The six men sat around the oval table, studying the restricted report. Satisfied that everyone had finished, the chairman of the group leaned back in his seat.

'The Saudis are furious this has come out, not surprisingly,' he said. 'But they've calmed down, realizing that it's in no one's interests to disturb the mutually beneficial prospects for growth and security over the next decade that our group has outlined. Besides, they need us as much as we need them.'

'What about Charles?' Redditch asked.

'What about him?'

'How is he?'

'He's fine. Being looked after. But there will be no electronic footprints from Charles which can be traced back to any of us. Nothing at all.'

Redditch nodded.

'But we're not out of the woods yet.'

A few shrugs.

'I'm sorry to report that Senator Harry Steinberg has made a formal request to my office, asking me to appear in front of his committee in a fortnight's time. Deborah Jones will also be giving evidence.'

The air-con unit growled low in the background.

'I think she's piecing this together. I've even heard whispers in the corridors of power that she's got a log of all my cellphone calls to Charles.'

Silence.

'I'm afraid, gentlemen, they're going to try and pick us off one by one. Unless . . .'

'Unless what?' asked Redditch.

'Unless one of us contacts Steinberg.'

'Steinberg? Why him?'

'He has the power. Influence. He alone can guide the committee. You know that.'

'What do you propose?'

The chairman opened his briefcase and handed round five copies of another restricted file. 'All men have secrets, they say. Some darker than others. Harry Steinberg is no different.'

Later that night, with the six men safely back on board the plane and heading to a global security conference in California, the chairman made a call to an unlisted number at an underground office fifteen miles south-west of Baltimore. It was an NSA number. 'Any update for me?'

'It's all in hand. We've got plenty on your Senator.'

The chairman clicked off the call. Then he leaned over and relayed the message to Redditch.

Redditch called up a number from his cellphone and sighed. 'Good evening, Senator. This is Bud Redditch, national security adviser. You fancy meeting up for lunch next week? My treat.' A pause. 'Great. How are the kids?' A pause. 'And Kathleen?' A pause. 'Of course, Senator. I look forward to that. Good night to you.'

He hung up.

The chairman stared out at the darkness.

'What contingency plans have you drawn up for Steinberg?'

'He's booked a seven-night break in Aspen ahead of the hearings. Very fond of off-piste skiing with his new intern, so I'm led to believe.'

Redditch closed his eyes and smiled. 'The *Enquirer*'s just gonna love that.'

Acknowledgements

I'd like to thank my editor, Paul Sidey, who not only helped me define the book, but was also a great sounding board as the story developed. Many thanks also to my agent, Caradoc King.

Special mention must go to Oxblood Ruffin, a technology expert and human rights activist, who gave me a couple of ideas about how to hack into a smartphone. In addition, the work of Seymour M. Hersh in the *New Yorker* magazine I found not only fascinating, but informative as I wrote this book. His portrayal of military and security matters in Iraq, and abuses inside Abu Ghraib, I found compelling. I also found 'Read Between the Lines of Those Missing 28 Pages' by Robert Scheer in *The Nation*, July 29, 2003, highly informative.

Many thanks also to Billy Martin in Washington DC and the experts at the Everglades National Park in Florida.

Regards to the great Ash Swanson and Stuart Chisholm in South Beach, and the regulars and irregulars at Mac's Club Deuce bar on 14th Street, Miami Beach. Not forgetting Melissa, Kenny and Colin.

Finally, my wife Susan and my two boys, Robbie and Ewan, for the inspiration and keeping me sane.

ALSO AVAILABLE IN ARROW

Beautiful Lies

Lisa Unger

Beware of who you trust . . .

When Ridley Jones steps off a New York street corner to save the
life of a young child, she is thrown into a whirlwind of violence,
deception and fear. And her world is turned upside down.

But just as she has a chance to pick up the pieces of her shattered
life, another seemingly ordinary act leads her into dark territory she
never knew existed, and where she must question everything she
knows about those close to her.

Forced to hunt down a ghost from the past, Ridley risks everything
and learns to trust no one in a race to find the truth before it finds
her . . .

arrow books

THE POWER OF READING

Visit the Random House website and get connected with information on all our books and authors

EXTRACTS from our recently published books and selected backlist titles

COMPETITIONS AND PRIZE DRAWS Win signed books, audiobooks and more

AUTHOR EVENTS Find out which of our authors are on tour and where you can meet them

LATEST NEWS on bestsellers, awards and new publications

MINISITES with exclusive special features dedicated to our authors and their titles

READING GROUPS Reading guides, special features and all the information you need for your reading group

LISTEN to extracts from the latest audiobook publications

WATCH video clips of interviews and readings with our authors

RANDOM HOUSE INFORMATION including advice for writers, job vacancies and all your general queries answered

Come home to Random House
www.rbooks.co.uk